Misplaced Mausoleum

A Novel

E.L. Buerger and K.S. Lorenz

iUniverse, Inc.
New York   Bloomington

This is a work of fiction. All of the characters, names, incidents,
organizations, and dialogue in this novel are either the products
of the author's imagination or are used fictitiously.

iUniverse books may be ordered through booksellers or by contacting:

iUniverse
1663 Liberty Drive
Bloomington, IN 47403
www.iuniverse.com
1-800-Authors (1-800-288-4677)

Because of the dynamic nature of the Internet, any Web addresses or links
contained in this book may have changed since publication and may no longer be
valid. The views expressed in this work are solely those of the author and do not
necessarily reflect the views of the publisher, and the publisher hereby disclaims
any responsibility for them.

ISBN: 978-1-4401-6781-2 (sc)
ISBN: 978-1-4401-6782-9 (ebook)
ISBN: 978-1-4401-6783-6 (dj)

Printed in the United States of America

iUniverse rev. date: 12/15/2009

DEDICATION

To the Readers with an imagination that enables them to enjoy this book by using their own thoughts, to visualize the characters as they see them. To select the towns, houses and places without having someone else describe them in detail.

TABLE OF CONTENTS

Chapter 1
THE MESSAGE

In his right hand, Pat held the message he found taped to the phone in his office. More than once, he had to remind himself not to drive over the speed limit. This was no time to have OFFICER MURPHY stop him. His parent's home was just a five-minute drive from his office. He would add fifteen or more minutes and he did not want to explain to Officer Murphy why he was in such a hurry.

As he turned along the winding curves on the road, he could see the house looming in the distance. It was a grand house, not a mansion, but nonetheless a large house. He turned in the direction of the garages and the parking area. He went straight to the front of the building, stopping at the foot of the stairs. Jumping out of the car, he ran up the stairs taking two at a time. JASON opened the door just as Pat reached the top landing. He held out his arms to stop Pat from colliding with him.

Jason yelled, "Pat. Pat. Stop, what is the matter? Did something happen to Mary or the boys?"

Pat was gasping for breath, not from racing up the long winding stairs but from holding his breath, as he drove to the house. He did manage to mouth, "Nothing is wrong with Mary or my boys. Where is my brother, is he hurt?"

Jason put his arm around Pat and ushered him into the foyer. He closed the large front door and headed for the small sitting room to the right.

Pat froze on the spot and yelled at Jason. "Why are you asking me what is wrong? What is the meaning of this?" He showed Jason the piece of paper he was still holding tightly in his hand. "Jason, I found this message taped to my phone when I returned to my office. What is so urgent to send for me ASAP? I came as fast as I could, you better not be playing one of your NASTY little games again." Seeing the puzzled look on Jason's face, he blurted out," I am sorry Jason; I know you would never use my bother as an excuse to get me to the house. I am concerned that Matt had some kind of accident."

Jason looked at the message, it read "Contact Jason immediately, concerning your brother."

"What the hell is this", replied Jason, "this is not the message I left. Now, now, Pat, simmer down. This really is not the message I left. Who is that Air Brain that answered your phone? I asked for MS. BENSON and this strange voice came on the line. It spoke in a robotic voice."

'Ms...Benson...is...not...available...do...you...wish...to... leave...a... message?

"I asked where you were. Again, it replied in that robotic voice."

'I…am…not…able…to…answer….that…question…Do…you…wish…to…leave…a…message…or…not…?'

"I told IT, just tell them Jason called and to return my call as soon as they return to the office.

My first reaction was that you had some new fangled recording on the phone and then IT said."

'Do…you…have…a…last…name…Jason…?'

"There was a tone of sarcasm in the voice. I told IT Mr. Hastings would know who Jason is.

By then I was getting annoyed. I told IT, I am afraid not too politely, that you both knew my number. IT asked me what the message was concerning. I am not sure but I may have yelled in the phone, "HIS BROTHER" and I slammed the phone down. I am accustomed to either you or Ms. Benson answering your phone, or the answering machine switching on with Ms. Benson's voice. Who is that twerp?"

Pat hunched his shoulders, "What about my brother, is he hurt or what?"

"Your brother is fine, physically at least, I am not sure about his mental capacity."

Hearing this, Pat felt a wave of relief surging through his body. Jason has been their mentor since they were both toddlers. Whenever he was, frustrated with either of them he referred to their mental capacity.

Pat asked Jason "Where is Matt now?"

"In the den with his nose glued to that computer. He sits there for hours on end. That is why I called your office. I did not want to speak to you. I wanted to talk to Ms. Benson. I have known both her and her late husband for many years. When I had a concern about raising you boys, I talked over my dilemma with her. She has given me sound advice through the years.

I realize you have been putting in many hours a week learning your new position. I also realize Matt is learning from ALAN WILSON just what his responsibilities will be when he takes over from him. I do not think Matt needs to put so many hours on the computer. I have to bring his meals into him. I just do not understand what is so hypnotic about that computer of his. It is not healthy to isolate oneself like that. He was at it until 2 A.M. this morning. I had to drag him off to bed. I felt I needed advice from Ms. Benson. So do you know who answered your phone?"

"I'm afraid so, her name if MAUREEN LANGLEY. We have had trouble with that girl on several occasions. Across the hall from my office is the records department and that is where she was moved to.

She began to come into the office and offer to help Ms. Benson. She said she had time on her hands and wanted to be useful. Ms. Benson told her she did not need her assistance and to leave our Private Office, as it was off limits to her. She persisted in annoying Ms. Benson.

At first, I did not mind her intrusion. She was kittenish and coy. However, when I heard her telling Ms. Benson that it was time for someone of her age to retire, I gave her orders not to enter our office again. I informed her she had no business being in there. I keep important financial records in the office.

I thought after the last run in Ms. Benson and I solved the problem by locking the door when we left the office.

I remember very well the last time I had trouble with her. I had asked my wife (Mary) to meet me for lunch. Mary had avoided coming to the office knowing how hectic my training with Ms. Benson was. As I came down the hall, there was my wife, running toward me. I could see she was furious. She yelled at me "Who is that Bitch in your office?"

Jason, you know Mary, she does not use such language. She told me the Bitch would not let her into my office, not only that but she was very nasty. Ms. Benson was returning to the office and overheard Mary.

Ms. Benson yelled, "Is that S. O. B. in the office. I will take care of her once and for all".

"I do not know what Benson did but the girl stayed away for several weeks. Then we began to notice strange things happening in the office. Both Benson and I have a habit of pushing our chairs into the desk and placing our phones for easy access. We started to find our chairs pushed back from our desks and the phones were on the other side of our work area. On one occasion, Benson asked me if I had looked at the folders on her desk. I told her I had no reason to".

"Well then, she said, someone has been in the office. These should be red on top, white in the middle and blue on the bottom. Now I find red on top, blue in the middle and the white on the bottom. I know I did not leave them that way. I think I will have our locks changed. We have had the same keys for quite some years now. Someone must have gotten one of the spare keys. I have a feeling that it is that Maureen Langley girl. You know she has been telling everyone that I am too old for the job. I think she wants to replace me."

I told Ms. Benson, at chance, nobody could do the job the way she does. I would be at a complete loss without her. She left the office saying she would have a talk with the Personal Manager, MR. PETERSON and review the girl's credentials.

When she returned, she had a satisfied look on her face. She told me Mr. Peterson showed her the girl's resume and letters of recommendation. They were very impressive. Yet her performance did not match the description in the letters. She was a troublemaker from the start. She did not know as much about the computers as stated in her resume.

Maureen started passing rumors about MARY ELLEN and JOHN PETERS, hinting they were having an affair. You know John; he is the fellow that had a horrible accident that left him handicapped. Mary Ellen has a devoted husband who just happens to be Peterson's nephew.

On the day, Maureen ran to Mr. Peterson to tell him that John and Mary left together and was going to have a 'Romantic Interlude'. Mr. Peterson knew Mary Ellen was on an errand for Peterson and John was going to the far side of the estate to see MARK DALEY on business for Peterson.

Peterson tried to fire her but she put up a stink, threatening to go to the Labor Board.

Mr. Peterson told Ms. Benson, "With our Mr. Wilson getting up in years, he does not need that kind of trouble. We are one big happy family here at the Park. We do not know how that rotten apple slipped through. She causes trouble in every department we place her in."

"All seemed to be going well until now. She must have convinced the Security Team to let her have a key, or she stole it when they were not looking. Ms. Benson said she asked JOHN WILSON to check Maureen's past employment history. He will use the Investigator from the Law Firm.

Jason, is not John Wilson, one of Alan Wilson's son? Why did he not choose one of his sons to take over his duties at the Park, instead he choose Matt.

"John and his brother went into Law. They are heading the Firm EDMOND WILSON, Alan's grandfather handed down.

Their grandmother, ANNIE, ran the Law Firm until her death. The boys worked with their grandmother, it was their desire to take over the Law Firm."

"Well for now, I will have Mr. Peterson assign Maureen to the Dance Studio with DANA, Pat said."

Jason threw up his hands and laughed, "You can't mean my cousin Dana. Good grief, Dana can be one tough person. She will have that girl polishing mirrors or waxing floors on her hands and knees. I have an idea! Dana and I were discussing what to do with all the old records kept in boxes in the storeroom. They must go back forty years or more. I will set up a computer in that storage room and Dana can have Maureen enter all the old records into the computer. If she dares to give Dana trouble, well, I would not want to be in her shoes."

Pat said, "I will have Ms. Benson call a Lock Smith and have new keys made for the office. Ms. Benson will have one, I will have one, and you will have one."

Jason asked, "What about the Security Department, don't they need keys for all offices?"

"I have a hunch she will try to get a copy of the new key from them. She can be very persuasive. If Security needs to get into the office, they can break the glass in the door. Good grief, I just remembered, Ms. Benson called me this morning saying she had to pick up the report from the Investigator. She said she would meet me at the office. I left before she got there, she must be wondering what happened. I will call her on the intercom and we can both fill her in about the message I found taped on my phone.

Ms. Benson answered the phone and began to question Pat. "Why did you run out of the office? I tried to call you but you were in such a hurry."

"I'm here with Jason, at my parents home, we are on the intercom and will fill you in on what happened."

After hearing the story, she said, "I have the report on that creature, you will not believe it. Maureen Langley is not only a Con Artist but the police want her and her partner. Apparently, she worms her way into the office of a very wealthy man and compromises him with her beguiling way and kittenish charms. That is why she wanted to get me to retire. Then she would have a clear path to use her devilish scheme on you.

The men she blackmailed were innocent but their companies could not afford the scandal. She received a pay off with large sums of money. The letter of recommendation was not genuine. Her partner would get a job in the company and type them on the Company Letter Heads."

Pat gasped, and told her about the plan to have Maureen transferred to the Dance Studio with Dana. Pat told her he would return to the office after seeing his brother Matt.

After hanging up the phone, he turned to Jason and asked what Ms. Benson's first name was. "I would feel foolish asking her. Matt and I have known her for so many years. As youngsters, we called her Ms. Benson. We never use her first name."

Jason said, "Of course I know it, it is Susan. As I said, I knew her husband. Both of them were my friends since college days. If I remember correctly, I introduced them to one another."

"My two boys call her Benny" Pat replied. "She thinks that is cute, so we let them call her Ms. Benny."

Jason and Pat sat there in the parlor for a while not saying anything. Suddenly Pat asked, "now that we have that message straighten out, what did you want to talk to Ms. Benson about concerning Matt?"

Jason said, "I was worried with your brother keeping held up in the den for days on end. He would not eat unless I brought his meals in to him. I personally still do not see what is so hypnotic about that computer of his."

Chapter 2
THE BROTHERS

Pat went to the Den and pushed the door open. "What is going on Matt? Jason seems really concerned."

This startled Matt, he turned so quickly he nearly knocked over the lunch tray that Jason had placed near him. "I tried to tell Jason I had lunch with Mr. Wilson but you know Jason, he set the tray down and before I could utter a word, he was out the door."

Jason was not exactly the standard butler. He had been with their family since they were very young. He was more like an uncle to both of them. He was their mentor, teacher, and caregiver.

The two brothers were 6 feet tall, Jason was 5'8", not that Jason was short but 4" made a difference as far as the boys were concerned. The two of them would stretch up as tall as possible, on their toes, then take out their combs. Pat ran his comb through his thick red hair, and Matt ran his comb through thick blond hair. They would then bend over and kiss Jason on his bald spot. Jason would turn and walk away mumbling just loud enough to let them hear him say. "Those Dirty little comedians." With his back to them, they could not see the grin on his face stretching from ear to ear, until one day they caught his reflection on a glass panel.

"Do not tell me he has been on your case too, Matt said to Pat. You know I have been having meetings with OLD MAN WILSON. It is too much to remember so I am trying to make sense of what he tells me by putting it in the computer. You will not believe what I have learned. I am not sure it is for real or just an Old man's confused mind."

"Need I remind you Matt; do not call him 'Old Man Wilson' in front of him."

"Not to worry, I made that mistake once and Jason nearly chewed my head off. Mr. Wilson is the last of the original members of the Foundation for the Park. He claims he has a dilemma and must decide if he should let the story die or pass it on to me."

"What story? Pat asked you mean the one about the SECRET in that building they call a mausoleum? Evidently, he has made up his mind. The two of you are having one meeting after another."

"Do you know where Jason is now?" Matt asked Pat.

"He went into town to make arrangements for our parents coming home next week. He has to open up the whole house."

"I forgot" Matt said "And how long have they been in Europe this time?"

Pat shrugged his shoulders, "I do not even remember which Embassy they were at. Well they never stay more than a week or so. I really do not think they come home to see us as much as to see the grandkids. That might be their reason for coming home. Or, just to entertain their friends. We know they throw lavish parties with Jason taking care of all the details. Then they can just be Host and Hostess.

By the way, did you ever get Mr. Wilson to talk to you about the position formally held by RICHARD BANKS that I know hold even though there are many men more qualified to tackle the job?

"It was not easy but I did manage to slip that question to him," Matt said. "He talks so fast on so many subjects. That man talks incessantly about the Park and his duties. I am never sure if he is serious or pulling my leg. He has an odd sense of humor. When the waiter brought our food I again mentioned that you were wondering why you were selected from all the highly skilled applicants that applied for the job."

He turned to me and said, "If that is all you want to know then I will say; it is imperative that the one selected possess a very special qualification."

Pat asked, "Do you remember, I mean what is your first recollection of just being in the Park?

Our parents have always been very busy (and absent) people, raveling all over the globe. Jason was in charge of us in their absence. I think he saw to it that we spent every waking hour in the Park. Probably to get rid of us, no I take that back, he loves the park too."

"What I really remember," Matt replied, "was how difficult it was to go off to college and leave all the good times behind. Here are the qualifications! Well Pat, unbelievably, our love for the Park is all it takes, plus our background in business. He is not looking for a Whiz Kid. He kept repeating, a deep-rooted love for the Park. He does not want someone using the job as a stepping stone to advance his career."

To that Pat said, "No problem, in our marriage vows Mary and I both stated that we would spend the rest of our lives right here. We have bought our home nearby. We want our children to know the same joys we shared growing up near the Park. Anyway, Mary's whole family lives in the area. We both like it right here, not to forget it is a stones throw from you and Jason.

Matt, I just thought of the first time we entered the forbidden Mausoleum with permission. That was an eerie experience. We were around 11 or 12 and DAN FARGO, (Alan Wilson's best friend and member of the Foundation) saw us trying to get a look inside. He just took us by the hand and led us in. I remember seeing that large table with all the chairs around it and the filing cabinets. He told us that was where the Board held their meetings. Do you remember those large pillars with the statues on top?"

"Pat, Mr. Wilson said they changed the meeting place to the Manor House when the Foundation members began to pass away. The office staff was getting larger and they needed more room. As you know, my meetings with Old Man Wilson are in the Mausoleum. The table is gone but the file cabinets are still there along with some very comfortable chairs. One of these days I may get to see the records kept in the file cabinets. That is, when he is satisfied that I am well grounded in Park Policies. I think what he is really waiting for is to decide if I can be trusted with some BIG SECRET. He keeps mentioning his DELIMMA."

"Well I do not know about you but I am content just having this job. It is the dream of my life to work for the Foundation. Now that I am one of the members, I do not give a hoot about some mysterious secret, if there even is one. What time did you say you are having your next meeting with Mr. Wilson?"

"I'm to meet him tomorrow, around noon at the Mausoleum. First, I will go to the office and retrieve some papers he left there. I will fill you in when I get back. Before I go I want to put the rest of these notes in the computer."

"That reminds me I told Jason I would ask why you spend so much time on the computer. What are you doing anyway?"

Matt removed a box from under the desk and showed it to Pat. He removed the lid revealing a large assortment of scraps of paper."

"Good grief Matt, do not tell me he has you going around with a stick picking up scraps of paper in the Park!"

Matt laughed, "No, no, these are the personal notes I have been keeping. He talks so much about his duties, the ones I am supposed to learn. I know I cannot remember them all so I make notes and put them into the computer. He skips around so much, one day he tells me about the Stables and then he changes the subject to something else; whatever enters his mind at the moment at first I kept a notebook, until he got irked and told me to put it away. He said people would think I am his secretary. He told me if he wanted a secretary it would be someone curvy, with long legs and a short skirt.

I cannot believe that I have been following him around for four months. He is so interesting and funny. Of course, I never know if he means what he says. There are times I am reminded of Jason."

Pat said, "I can believe that, one time he came into the office and started to tease Ms. Benson behind my back. I though it was Jason until I turned around and saw him standing there.

Does he know you have all those notes?"

"No I write them in private, I go to the men's room quite often. By the time, I return home my pockets are full. When he goes to talk to someone, I hurry and write on a napkin. Fortunately he has not said anything to let me know he suspects what I am doing."

Pat told Matt it would be a good idea to let Jason in on the big secret whatever it turns out to be. He said, "If we do not, he will not let either of us have any peace. We have never kept any secrets from him. Jason has been our confidant since we learned to talk. I would trust him with my life and so would you. However, I am not sure this is the right time to fill him in. You know as well as I, when Jason starts talking we are stuck listening to him for hours reciting his deep love, fond memories and his loyalty for the members of that Foundation."

"Not to worry, I happen to know that he has a date to go riding with John and RUTH Wilson. (They are Alan Wilson's second son and daughter in-law). They will be going out to dinner after riding.

Jason and Dan, (one of the original founders) were very close. Jason will know if there is any basis to what Alan Wilson is saying or as you suspect just an Old Man's imagination. I am sure he is beside himself wanting to know what we are discussing. I thought I heard him come in. Matt opened the door to the den and called out to Jason. Jason, old buddy, come in, sit down and make yourself comfortable. We have a problem that only you can solve. Tell us all you know about Alan Wilson. Can we trust him, or is he just an old fool? Our future depends on his honesty. He keeps referring to a DELIMMA, but will he say what it is?"

Jason just stood there with his hands on his hips staring at both boys. He finally spoke, "I do not know what you two upstarts have been up to lately, you have taken your time letting me into your confidence. I have been proud of you both getting into the Foundation. Now it seems there is much more involved than I have been lead to believe. I do not mind telling you both I have been rather pissed at your secrecy. I know you both have to stand on your own in making decisions. I would not interfere and you both know that. Therefore, you want to know about Mr. Wilson. OK. For starters, if you try not to interrupt, I will tell you all I know.

Let me start by telling how I happened to become a family member of the Park Staff. MATHEW! I will not tell you again. Stop fiddling with that computer; I will not utter another word until you do. That is more like it. Turn it off. Sit over there by Pat. Jason, looking at both boys began.

Chapter 3
JASON'S STORY

When I was quite young, probably eight, my Dad was head maintenance man for a large outfit. My Mother had passed away and dad's duties did not leave enough time for him to spend caring for me. We had several nannies but they were not nice. Some were down right nasty. They complained to my dad about my behavior. He thought it was because I was still grieving for my mother.

The last one was meaner than the rest. If I remember correctly her name was NAVARE something or other. Her daughter had the habit of punching me in the ribs. When I pushed her hand away, she would throw up her arms and scream to her mother that I hit her. The mother made me sit in the corner for hours. Sometimes the daughter would hit me on the back of my head. I dared not complain. If I had to go to the bathroom, she would never allow me to get off the chair.

One day my dad came home early. He discovered me locked in a corner closet while the woman and her children were eating the treats he brought for all of us. Her son ran for the key to unlock the closet. I heard my dad's voice and called out to him. Dad grabbed the key and unlocked the door.

The woman always blamed me for things her daughter did. I would have like to play with some of her son's games but she would not let me. He not only played with mine, he would break them and blamed it on me.

When Dad realized I was telling the truth about being put in the closet as a form of punishment he threaten to have her arrested for child abuse. Dad did go to the police and file a report on the woman. He did not want her to abuse another child as she did me. The woman's husband apologized to my dad. He promised that his wife would never take care of any other child again. Her husband said his wife had a blind eye where her own children were concerned.

Then Dad learned of a job opening at a large estate in the suburbs. The owners were making the estate into a Park. Since my dad was a maintenance man for a large organization, he felt he could handle his new job. He talked to Dan Fargo and got the job. Dan said we could live in the Manor House. That is what he called it. There were so many rooms. We would have a place to call our own.

Dan, his wife CLAUDIA and MARGO, the elder member of the Foundation had their own living quarters on the second floor. Dad must have told them of my ordeal. They sure went out of their way to make me feel wanted.

Claudia insisted I call her Aunt Claudia, and then Margo said she would be Grandma Margo. Of course, Dan became 'Uncle' Dan.

The first time I met Alan Wilson he scared me half to death. He heard me call out 'Uncle' Dan; he grabbed me by the arm and shouted, "You can not call him Uncle Dan unless you call me Uncle Alan. Then he got down on his knees and hugged me. He stood up with me in his arms and twirled me around. He went on to say he had two boys that were my age, one 7 and the other 8. He promised to bring them to meet me. He told Dan that he had a long talk with my dad and that my dad told him it would be all right for him to bring me to meet the others at the Dance Studio. I met RENEE, and MICHAEL and their three girls. They were ages 3, 4 and 5. Alan introduced me as their new cousin.

He did keep his word; I met his sons JOHN and EDDIE. We spent many happy hours together. We called ourselves the 'SIX COUSINS'. Can you imagine, an eight year old with only his dad and nasty housekeepers suddenly having a whole family, a Grandmother, Aunts, Uncles and Cousins.

Aunt Claudia and Grandma Margo insisted that dad and I have our meals with them. When dad had to work late, Grandma Margo would take me to my room and read to me until I fell asleep. If dad had to leave early for work, one of them came to get me and fixes my breakfast then takes me to school.

I cannot say that was the happiest year of my life because each year became better. Uncle Alan would take the three boys and sometimes the three girls to the stables to go riding. As you both know, I am an excellent rider. You have seen my ribbons.

In addition, of course, there was Aunt KATHY and UNCLE RICHARD. He is the member of the Foundation that held the position you now have Pat. One time they took all six of us cousins on a Cruse Ship. They had no children of their own. Uncle Alan had permission from my dad to take me to his house on some weekends to be with John and Eddie. I met Papa Wilson (Edmond) and Grandma Annie. They treated me just like one of their very own grandsons. I also got to meet Aunt Louise and Uncle Frank. She worked with Papa at the Investment Firm. Frank worked for Grandma Annie at the Law Firm. Sometimes GRACE, Frank and Louise's granddaughter would be there.

My dad had a heart attack and passed away. He lived long enough to see me graduate from High School. The family considered me still part of it. I too attended college with Uncle Alan's boys. Uncle Alan told me that nothing would change. Eddie became a Lawyer John was torn between coming a Lawyer and going into the Financial Business. I of course as you know, became an educator. I taught in a private school out of state but I was not happy. I missed my family and the Park. My girl friend had dumped me for someone else. Uncle Dan heard of this and sent for me to come home.

Your family needed someone to take charge of their two little ones while they were off on some of their Social or Political affairs. The nanny was not up to doing the job full time. Dan and Alan were friends of your grandfather they suggested me. It was my duty to entertain and discipline. NANNY got the dirty job of feeding, cleaning, etc. I had the enjoyable part.

I planned to continue living at the Manor House and going to your house every morning. That did not last long. After the fourth or fifth time having Nanny wake me to tell me, "Your boys are up and horsing around. They will not stay in bed. Come over at once and take care of YOUR BOYS." I would go over to find that you were just unhappy little guys. Your parents were off somewhere. You were just lonesome. I remembered how it was when my dad worked late and I was alone with a nasty housekeeper. Maybe it was the way she said, 'YOUR BOYS' I realized you were my boys. I got permission from your grandfather to move in permanently.

Dan and his wife Claudia lived in the Manor House for many years. Alan and his wife EVE lived in the city. Eve worked in the Investment Firm with Papa. Alan's father ROBERT worked in the Law Firm. Alan oversaw the daily workings of the Park, while Dan was more interested in the riding stables.

I did ask Dan on occasion, why they built the Mausoleum in such an off spot. He managed to skirt around the answer but he did say no one wanted the Mausoleum to be his or her resting place. He passed my questions off by saying something to the effect that they could not get a permit from the county.

Jason looked at Matt, then Pat, "I will tell you both once and for all, my Uncle Alan is an honorable man. You can take him at his word. If he says, there is a secret you can believe it. I will admit he is also a jokester. He loves to pull a leg or two. You do learn to tell the difference between his humor and his seriousness.

I remember well the time he called the three boys, John, Eddie and me into his office.

Uncle Dan was looking at some papers in the corner of the room with his back to us. Uncle Alan said he was at an inspection of a plant that makes soda pop and recently returned. He told us he was shocked to see so many roaches near the sugar stacks. He looked so somber when he told us "You would not believe it without seeing it with your own eyes. There were two giant roaches carrying a 50-pound sack of sugar on their backs." This story fascinated us until we spotted Uncle Dan leaving the room. He was trying hard not to laugh in front of us. We could see he was doubling up and holding his sides. Uncle Alan would tell us ridiculous stories to teach us not to believe everything we heard. He wanted us to think for ourselves. The possibility of roaches being that big was imperceptible. Yet we believed his every word.

I will repeat again, Alan Wilson is an honorable man. Matt will you let me know the secret as soon as you get an answer?

Jason stood up abruptly, turned from them and stated. "Since I seem to be boring you both, I will leave."

Both Matt and Pat learned (from years of experience) that he did not really think he was boring them; it was just his way to get their attention. They snapped to and said, "Aye, Aye Sir."

Matt looked at the clock on the wall and said, "My goodness will you look at the time. Jason you will be late for your date with John and Ruth. We have kept you long enough. You run along and I will let Cook 1 know that you will not be here for dinner."

As Jason took off, the two brothers looked at one another. Pat said, "Nice going, I will be off too. I left the office in such a hurry. What are your plans?"

"I will copy the rest of these notes into the computer. With Jason gone I will be able to get my thoughts together for tomorrow when I meet with Mr. Wilson. I sure have a great deal of respect for him now that Jason filled us in on the type of person he really is."

Pat turned at the door and called to his brother, "Do not forget to tell Cook."

Matt replied, "Are you kidding? She told me of his date with John and Ruth. Let me know the out come on that Maureen person"

"Tell you what, Pat replied, I will call Ms. Benson before I leave. Where do you keep the phone? Never mind, I see it peeking out from under that pile of papers."

Pat hung up the phone after his call and said, "We will not be bothered with the likes of her anymore. The police have her and her partner. They are taking them off to California to stand trial for crimes they committed there. The Wilson's Investigator had contacted the California police, based on his investigation. He gave the report to Ms. Benson. We will not be involved in that mess. I will keep you informed on the details after your meeting with Mr. Wilson tomorrow."

Chapter 4
THE SECRET DOOR

The next morning as Matt drove up the long road leading to the Manor House, he saw the lush green grass that seemed to stretch for miles. He steered the car to the parking area used by the office staff.

There had been a side entrance installed for security. Mr. Wilson's car was nowhere in sight. Perhaps, he thought, his son dropped him off at the front door.

Matt entered the door and stepped into the foyer. Directly in front of the entrance was a small private elevator leading to the second floor. To the left he saw the fire door exit to the picture gallery. He turned to the right and went down the long corridor. At the end sat the Security Guard at a table. The Park was open to the public but not the offices.

Matt went into Alan Wilson's office to retrieve the papers he requested. They were in a brief case on the desk. To Matt's surprise, the case was very, very old.

Once back in his car, Matt drove to the other side of the building. He thought, as often as I have been here, I did not realize the length of this building, until now. When he approached the back of the building, he saw Mr. Wilson sitting on the marble bench that was just outside of the building. Evergreens surrounded the bench giving a Post Card look at the old man sitting there. He was holding what looked like a metal pipe in his hand. Mr. Wilson got up and stepped forward holding out the object to Matt. "I have been waiting for you young man"

Matt asked, "How did you get here? I did not see your car. Did John or Eddie bring you out here? I know they get upset when you drive out from the city."

"So, I am pushing ninety, I can still drive. It is just that the traffic is so damn crowded. I stayed here last night in Dan's old apartment. When Dan was having trouble with his legs there was a small elevator put in near the winding staircase. Dan has been gone these past six months. The apartment is in good condition. John put up a fuss about me staying here. I told him Jason was only a five-minute drive away. The night cleaning crew were going to be downstairs working in the Picture Gallery all night. That did not satisfy him. He called Jason to inform him of my plans. The next thing I knew, Jason was here with his over night bag. He spent the night in Margo's old room."

"Jason is here? No wonder he was not bugging me to have breakfast this morning. Where is he now?"

"Fast asleep, I checked in on him before I came down. He was up half the night; talking to the cleaning people. I think he was going through some of the collections. He used to do that with Dan. It was like old times having him here. Dan's kitchen window overlooks the front drive. I saw you drive in and went down to the kitchen. They will have breakfast ready for us when we return to the house."

"Then we will not be here long at the Mausoleum. What is that object you are carrying?"

"This is a key to that heavy door. I had planned to play a trick on you concerning this phony key, but Jason tells me I have gone too far giving you the run around with my duties here at the Park. He asked me to COOL IT.

I decided months ago that you would be taking over my duties. I did not want to hand the job to you on a silver platter. I wanted you to appreciate the seriousness of all that the duties entail. Jason had set up my schedule from January through December. You can shred all those scraps of paper you have been so diligently keeping. I suppose in your eyes, I am a dirty old man. And rightly so, but I did enjoy it.

Take a good look at this key; it is really a metal pipe with two small pieces welded to one end and an ornate handle to the other. When the Mausoleum was near completion, we wanted a door for the Mausoleum to be strong so no one could break into it and vandalize the Mausoleum. We were afraid our secrets would be uncovered. Afraid, no terrified was how we all felt, especially the woman.

We asked our locksmith to give us something that would deter anyone from breaking in.

This monstrosity is what we got. Come I will give you a demonstration. First, I push the key in the lock two inches and give it a turn. Then another two inches and turn the key in the opposite direction. Another two inches and bring it back down again. Finally give it a push until you hear a click. The door swings open. It is not the key that does it. Our locksmith had one two many pranks played on him by Dan and I. That was his way to get even.

Did you notice, as I worked the key, my other hand was on the side decoration. That is one of our secrets. There are many more secrets for you to learn. I was pushing a button built into the frame of the decoration. Come inside and close the door behind you".

Alan pulled a small key from his pocket and unlocked a panel box next to the front door jam.

He opened it and told Matt to watch as he pulled a lever down.

"This deactivates the outside button".

Matt said, "Now I am confused, why would you deactivate the button from the inside. Is that not defeating the purpose of the outside button? Is it not used to keep people from using it and gaining entry"?

"That is another secret. Stand facing the room from here and tell me exactly what you see. I know this is not your first time in the Mausoleum, but look closely. I want you to really see what is here".

Matt stared for a while and said, "Well the room is about 30 feet wide and 40 feet long. There are four statues on the left side, a double statue at the back and three statues on the right. There are two stuffed chairs in front of us with a table between and a file cabinet".

"Bright boy, now describe the statues".

"Ok, they all stand on a base three feet high. The statue is around five feet high. The first is a statue of the Bard, Shakespeare, the second is a Ballerina, and the third is a Musical Instrument. The fourth is an Angel of some kind. At the far end it looks like two boys with arms entwined. Next is a man dressed in riding gear. Then there is another one holding a pen. There looks like a desktop on his lap and what looks like an ink well. The last one is looking through binoculars. As I see it, the first three represent the Theater, the Dance Studio and the Music Studio. I do not understand the purpose of the angel. What does the Angel represent"?

"That is our Fairy Godmother, Margo. The boys represent Charles Fargo and Edmond Wilson, our Papa. The one with the riding crop represents the Stables. The middle one represents our accountant. Finally yet importantly is the Overseer. With the size of those binoculars, everything would be in sight for miles around. Put the brief case on the table next to the key and come with me."

Alan Wilson went to the middle statue. He told Matt to take hold of the ring finger and the pinkie on the hand touching the ink well. Move them in opposite directions, "

Matt did as instructed but nothing happened.

No, no, do not grab them like that. Hold each one gently; the ring finger goes back, and the pinkie goes forward. You must do this simultaneously.

Matt tried it again; he let out a yell and jumped back. The statue began to turn, leaving an opening between the statue and the back wall.

Alan Wilson went to the back and he entered through the opening. Matt slowly followed him. To Matt's surprise, he saw that the marble wall was almost three feet thick. There was plenty of lighting once Mr. Wilson turned on a switch. On the other side was a landing with three steps leading upward. To the left was a gate with stairs going down. Matt asked where the stairs going down led. Alan said they led to an old wine cellar. On this side was the bolt to the cellar door. On the other side in the cellar there was a rack hiding the door. He told Matt "We are going up, just follow me".

At the top of the three stairs was another landing that turned to the left. Then three more stairs, another landing, and three more stairs that turned to the right. At the top of these stairs Alan moved a plate in the wall and looked inside," Well, he said, it looks like the Library is empty".

Matt did not see what Alan did but the panel in the wall opened. They entered behind a very large desk. Matt thought, (well here are two more secrets to tell Pat and Jason. Matt saw a long table in the center of the room where they met for the board meetings.

Alan went to the far side of the room in the Library with Matt close behind.

"This door he said is always kept locked. It is not open to the public." On the outer side of the Library door hung a large sign reading PRIVATE.

Matt looked at the very large Planter setting next to the staircase. He asked him how old the Planter was.

"Probably as old as the house, it contained various trees and plants through the years.

When Dan and I were very young we would hid behind the plant from his evil cousin VINEE. There is a door under the staircase. We used to pretend the original owners used it as a fast get-a-way from the police. We learned much later that it really was".

Before Matt could get in another question, Alan was on his way in the direction of the kitchen. Upon entering, they saw Jason sitting at one of the tables having his coffee. He motioned to them to come join him.

"Well, how did it feel to sleep in Grandma Margo's old room? Did it bring back memories of your youthful days Alan asked Jason"?

"You bet it did. I remembered the nights when the storms were very loud. She would come, get me from my room when dad was off on some work assignment, and bring me to her room. I felt so secure in her presence. I went into my old room, the one that dad and I shared. It is so bare now. When I went to live at the Hastings house, I took all the furniture with me. The mementos of my mom and dad were very important to me. I still have the large painting of my mother hanging in my room. Oh! There are some things left, but nothing that I would want".

Matt said to Jason, so that is a painting of your mother, Pat and I wondered who she was".

Jason became angry, "When did you boys enter my room? You knew that your parents were very strict. They insisted that I not let you in my quarters".

"Not to worry Jason, you were not around and they never knew. Do you really think two inquisitive boys would not be curious? Cook knew but she never let on".

"I will have a word or two with her. We both could have been fired".

Alan, realizing Jason was getting upset, changed the subject. He turned to Jason and asked, "Did you get out to the stables yesterday"?

Jason brightened up immediately. "I wanted to tell you about the two new horses arriving. You retired so early that I thought it best not to wake you. They are of exceptional quality.

You will be pleased when you see them. I have named them already. The white mare is beautiful. Her name is Princess Rose. The colt is dark brown. I named him Dudley. They will work well as stable horses".

Matt looked surprised, "You named the horses"?

I have been naming the horses since I was a young lad. When Papa's horse and Grandma Annie's were retired, I was very upset. I thought they were going to the glue factory. That is what I had heard would happen to old horses. Papa told me that would never happen to any of their horses. He told me he would have them cremated and their ashes spread in the meadow over the area they where ridden. The pasture is where our horses will be turn out to when they are too old to be ridden. Oh course they return to their stalls every night on their own".

"Yes said Alan, Dan and I both spread the ashes of Jake and Jimmy, our two faithful horses. They lived well beyond the normal life span of horses. We did not get other horses to replace them. We could not bring ourselves to do it. That was a year or so before Dan himself passed away. With Dan's poor legs and our advancing age, we just gave up riding.

Jason I want you to know I did give a few of our secrets to Matt. Did you have his key for the library door made yet? If not, do not worry, he will not need it just yet. You looked a little perturbed when we came in. Do you have a problem we should know about?"

"Not really, I received a call from EMMA. Pat had been trying to reach me. Emma said Pat wants to have a meeting with her and myself this afternoon.

She sounded concerned. I told her he must have gotten the guest list for the Hastings's party next week. I had planned to take her to the market to stock up on supplies for the big event. She feels it is more than just a chat. We will find out soon enough. Well I will be on my way. You two have fun! By the way, if you plan to stay here, there are no supplies in the upstairs apartment. There is not even decent drinking water. Do you want me to take care of that detail"?

"No, I will only be here a few days. Just long enough to work with Matt. I was thinking of going to the stables this morning with Matt. You run along and learn what Pat is up to".

Chapter 5
LOVE AND RESPECT

After finishing breakfast, Matt and Alan headed to the Library. When they reached the large planter near the door, Alan stopped for a moment remembering how full the plant was when he and Dan hid behind it. He made a mental note to himself to have that sickly tree removed and changed to a full blooming bush.

They entered the Library and headed toward the bookcase at the far end of the room. Alan opened the secret passage. Half ways down Alan stopped and asked Matt if he was excited about his parents coming to visit.

"No, not really, you must have met our biological parents at one of their parties. Pat and I do not ever remember spending time alone with either of them. They were not what you would call loving parents. We equate the names Jason and father to be the same.

Our grandfather (John Peters) died when we were about ten. He was a loving man. He played games with us and told us stories. We really miss him. Jason, Nanny and Cook gave us an abundance of love and attention".

Alan turned to Matt and said, "I was wondering, what your feelings were concerning them. I remember how upset Jason would become when they did not return home when one of his little boys became ill. He had such a loving father and family. He expected your parents to react the same. Instead they would tell him that he was in charge and to take care of the illness; that was what they were paying him to do".

At the bottom of the stairs, they entered the door leading to the Mausoleum. Alan motioned for Matt to sit on one of the overstuffed chairs. Alan closed the entrance door and sat in the chair next to Matt. "I did not ask what you thought of our parents out of idle curiosity. The original members of the Foundation were not all related by blood. Nonetheless, we could not have loved or respected one another more if we had been. Our secret has a great deal to do with our mutual love for one man. That man was Papa Wilson. I want you to read his story and learn why we loved him enough to keep a secret all these years.

First, I will tell you how this story came about. I also need you to learn about each member of the Foundation. I want you to know their characters and personalities to the extent that you feel you have known them all of your life.

I was working on a case for a client when I received a call from my wife Eve. She was not making any sense. All I could make out was that Papa was in the hospital. Without hesitation, I rushed right over to the hospital. When I got there, she was crying nonstop. I did not know if Papa was dead or had an accident. After I managed to calm her down, she told me Papa passed out at the office. Then she rambled on about some papers and the file cabinet that belonged to Charles Fargo, Papa's best friend. After what seemed like hours, Papa's doctor came down the hall. He held up his arms and said, "There is nothing physically wrong with the old man. His vital signs and mental state are fine. The only thing that seems to bother him is he cannot remember what transpired the last 24 hours. What ever happened to him must have been a tremendous shock to cause him to black out in such a manner. He is arguing with every one to let him go home. It would be wise to find out what shocked him. Can you convince him to stay at least overnight? If you can get him to tell you the last thing he does remember, perhaps that will help. I do not want him to become depressed. He is such an active man".

I went in to see Papa; he looked like his normal self, except for the memory loss. It took a great deal of persuasion on my part, but I finally convinced him to start a memory Journal. I told him I would have it recorded for him. I suggested he start with the very first thing he remembers. I told him to go back into his childhood. He implied I might find that boring. I said the doctor I spoke to suggested this as an easy way to find out what revelation, if any, had shocked him. It may help him to remember those missing hours. At the least, it will be something to pass on to the children. Then I reminded him how much we all loved him.

I went back to Eve; she was talking to Louise, and Frank. Louise had been Papa's private secretary for many years, now retired. Frank, her husband worked with our Grandmother, Papa's wife. They had been a foursome for many years. When Grandma Annie passed away, they seemed to drift apart. I asked Louise if there was some way she and Frank could keep Papa from returning to the office for at least a week. She said she would work on it.

The doctor had given Eve something to relax her. I told her I would be going to the airport to meet Dan.

MAX, grandma's private investigator said he had notified Dan with the news concerning Papa's situation. Max was my father's best friend. Grandma had treated him like a son.

Dan had gone to California at Papa's request. Vinnie, Dan's cousin, had fallen from his balcony and died instantly. At least that is what the police report stated. Papa wanted more information and sent Dan to investigate fully. Papa wanted Dan to prepare a report for Charlie when he returned home from his expedition.

The news of Vinnie's death did not sadden any of us. It just seemed too easy. I mean, Vinnie had so many enemies, people he hurt. If someone did him in, we wanted to know and shake his or her hand. If you had known Vinnie, you would understand.

Next stop was the private airport where we housed our company plane. It was due to land and I went out to meet Dan. As he disembarked, he staggered; my first thought was that there had been a mishap in the air. I saw Dan holding a paper and waving it at me. It was the telegram Max sent to Dan. I gave him our secret signal that all is well. He repeated the sign and so did I. He looked pale and stunned. I asked, "What did Max put in that damn telegram"?

He replied, "Max sent this? I should have known, I should have known. Only Max would do a thing like this. When I first read the damn thing, all I saw was Wilson, Wilson, and Wilson, Attorneys at Law. Then I saw Papa ill. Come home. It was signed Wilson.

This is one lesson I will never forget again. Max told me never look with my emotions, to see the facts that are in front of me. Look at this telegram! It reads Papa ill question mark. STOP. You knew I was on my way home. However, look it says "immediately question mark. STOP." None of this makes sense, especially the signature. Wilson, it should have been signed with the name of one of the family members. I tell you again, this is one lesson I will never forget. Do not for one second let on to Max the condition I was in when you saw me".

As I already mentioned, Max was Grandma Annie's Private Investigator for the Law Firm for many years. He was my dad Robert's age. Grandma treated him like one of her own.

When Max retired he still kept going to the Law Firm to be of help. The only life he knows was law. When he realized Dan was interested in following in his footsteps, he took him under his wings. Teaching him the things, you learn from experience, not from textbooks. This was one of those lessons. It came in handy to both of us later.

On the drive to the office, Dan filled me in on what he discovered during his trip to California. A few strange incidents puzzled him. Dan learned a girl named Kathy was working for Vinnie on his latest show production as a costume designer. We did not know that Vinnie was directing his own company. Vinnie learned from the Bar Man next to the theater that this girl was getting married. She had arranged for someone to take her place. Vinnie considered this as personal rejection. There was more to the story but Dan did not have time to investigate. For some unexplainable reason he felt he knew her.

Then there was Renee, a local girl from right here in town. We had heard rumors that pertained to her when Vinnie tried to rape her. He did not know that she was in California, but she was there when Vinnie had his accident.

At Vinnie's Condo, a neighbor heard a woman fighting with him on the day he fell and told Dan of the fight. She said Vinnie was yelling some very nasty things at the woman. She also said Vinnie was in one of his drunken rages. The neighbor showed him a picture of the woman standing next to her. Her niece had taken the picture thinking she was a friend. The woman was in tears and the neighbor tried to console her. The picture showed them both talking. Dan recognized the woman. She was a friend of Claudia. They were in the local theater group in our town. Her name was Margo; I believe a girl named Kathy had been working with them.

We decided to let that information ride until after viewing the papers in Papa's office. We were more certain than ever that whatever caused Papa to receive such a shock had to do with those papers he brought back from the Manor. We wanted to remove them before he returned to the office.

Matt, I am getting ahead of myself. I really want you to read Papa's story. He after all is the reason there is a secret. Alan Wilson got up, went to the back of the room. He stood in front of the figures of the two boys. Then he pushed down one gold leaf, put his finger in a hole and a drawer came forward. He retrieved a large folder. (Matt thought to himself, another secret! I wonder how many there are.) Alan went back to Matt, picked up the brief case and put the folder inside. "Take good care of this. I do not want it to get into any hands other than yours. If you have, any questions ask Jason. You will notice Louise is the Author. There is a good reason for that. Papa's story would have been very dull without her input.

Your car is out front. Take me to the stables and drop me off before you go home and start reading".

"How will you get back? It is too far from the stables for you to walk".

"Do not worry about me. I will have LARRY or a stable hand drive me back".

Matt asked. "Will you be staying at the Manor tonight? If so, I guess Jason will join you".

"Knowing Jason he probably has a large amount of supplies stocked in Dan's old apartment by now. I will be going home tomorrow. My son John is picking me up. They have some type of party planned for the family. I will return back here after that affair in my own car. Driving round here should not be too strenuous on my old bones. I suspect that John will drive me in my car. Ed will follow in his. He will have some excuse about going over the books with Pat. I wonder what your brother wanted with Jason and Emma".

(Matt wondered who Emma is).

Chapter 6
DECEPTION

Jason arrived home before Pat. He asked Emma the cook to join him in the den. "Just what did Pat have to say, he asked her"?

"He said he wanted to have a conference with the two of us. He sounded so serious. When I talked to Mary, she said he had been to see MR. McDONALD yesterday. Is he not the one in charge of the boy's inheritance? Do you think it has anything to do with their finances? Pat went to see MR. Mc Donald again this morning. I am worried. I love those boys as though they are my own."

"We will know soon enough. I hear his car."

Upon entering, the den Pat went straight to Emma and said "Hello Mother Emma". He turned to Jason and said, "I have many questions to ask of you. Why were we never to call Emma by her name Jason? Your many Aunts and Uncles we have known them quite well but you insisted we call them Mr. or Mrs."

"That was your parent's instructions, not mine. We were to treat Emma as an employee. They were very precise in those orders. The two of you were never to enter my rooms. They stated that the only relatives you had were your Grandfather, a Mother and a Father, no one else. If we wanted to keep our jobs, we had to abide by those rules. This was a hard thing for all of us to do. Your parents only came home two or three times a year, on your birthdays and the holiday at Christmas time. Many times, they arrived just hours before your Grandfather PETER MARTIN. This gave him the impression that they had been here for days. They showed both of you affection in front of your grandfather. As soon as he left, they were gone. We were afraid if we showed you boys affection in front of them, we would lose our jobs.

We loved both of you too much to let that happen. Why now, are you concerned with that?"

"I have been with Mr. McDonald, as you both know, Mary confided to me that she told Emma. Mr. McDonald told me he wants to retire; he feels he is too old to continue working. Grandfather Martin entrusted him with his will. He wanted to go over the assets with me. He had me read the Will. It reads that when the youngest grandson reaches the age of thirty, both boys will have charge of all assets. You know our ages.

I was shocked to learn that our mother and father will have no say whatsoever on the handling of anything. Mother will get a yearly allowance as long as Matt and I agree. He was very unhappy to discover that the lavish parties they were throwing here at the house were not for our birthdays. He was paying the bills for those parties. Mother and father never invited him so he just assumed that the parties were for us boys. Avis (mother) intimated that seeing him would remind the boys of their dear departed grandfather. He abided by her wishes.

Mr. McDonald was a trusted friend and confidant of Grandfather. They had been together for many years. Grandfather learned of having a daughter when she showed up at his door. She was eighteen and had come here from Europe. He recalled going to a Grand party many years before when he was nineteen. As he recalled, there was liquor served. He remembered waking up, not knowing how he got to bed.

He did not remember the girl's mother. Avis said her mother married into a well to do family. (It seemed that Avis was a spoiled rotten girl). Before her mother died, she told Avis that her real father was a wealthy American. She decided to come to America and confront him. Grandfather had blood test taken. The test showed the possibility of a relation to her. His cousins were at the party. There was not positive proof he fathered her. He let her come live with him, just incase she was his daughter. Avis had a boy friend that your grandfather disliked. All they wanted to do was attend parties. Avis married this GEORGE HASTINGS without approval from your grandfather. He refused to adopt her making her heir to his fortune.

George Hastings told Peter that Avis was expecting his grandchild. Peter told her she would get a hefty alliance if he could raise the child himself. To get the money, Avis agreed. George insisted that they live with his family in Europe until the baby was born. They sent pictures of the child to Peter instead of returning home as promised. They remained in Europe another year. When they did come back, they had two boys. One was thirteen months and the other an infant.

Mr. McDonald told Pat that Peter Martin loved his grandsons. When he saw that Avis and George were neglecting the boys he hired people he trusted to care for them. That was Jason, Emma and MARY WILSON (no relation)

That is not the half of it; Pat told them Mr. McDonald was puzzled at the actions of Avis and George. After Peter passed away, he had his investigator back track their where about during their supposed stay in Europe. What he came up with was unbelievable. They were not in Europe all that time. They were somewhere in California, living with a cousin of George. His cousin was not doing too well financially. He and his wife had a son, an infant. The wife was pregnant again. Soon after the second child was born, George's cousin and his wife disappeared. That was about the same time George and Avis returned to Peter Martin with 'their sons'. The Investigator could not find proof of foul play. Avis had the baby's birth certificates. It would have been easy for her to doctor up the names ARIES and GREG to look like Avis and George. The place of birth was a name they had not heard of.

You see Jason; they are not our parents after all. Mr. McDonald said he tried for years to find the real parents. The only thing they could verify was that Aries and Greg left for Europe with their sons. He was able to find plane records that read a Mr. and Mrs. Hastings and two sons on a flight to Europe. In addition, records of a return flight to America.

When Avis and George called Grandfather to tell him that they were flying to America they asked would he please meet them at the airport; he was overjoyed. There no questions asked.

Mr. McDonald said we would not be hearing from Avis or George ever again. He threatened them with criminal action for their personal use of our money. Grandfather had held huge birthday celebrations for each of our birthdays. The holidays were elaborate affairs. This is what Mr. McDonald assumed Avis and George were doing, continuing the custom. He blamed himself for not investigating. That dear man offered to mortgage his assets to repay us for the cost of those parties. The information he just gave me more than repays all expenses. Just knowing they were not our real parents would please Matt as well as me. To know that Jason and Emma will be with us for as long as they wish is a dream come true. I put him in contact with John and Eddie Wilson. He will transfer all our accounts to them. He really is a wonderful person. I told him our doors would be open to him and his family.

Emma, do you remember an incident that occurred when I was but a teen? It was at one of those huge parties the Hastings gave. I came running to you all upset. You told me to see Jason right away. He would make things all right. Jason told me to find Matt, go to our room, and play a game of Chess. Jason said he and you would come to us as soon as all those people left. When you did come to our room, I could not tell you why I was so upset. I am ready to tell you now.

I went to seek our 'mother' to ask her a question. Before I could utter a word she turned to the woman she was talking to and said, "This is one of my husband's sons." Then she turned and walked away with her guest. I then went to find my 'father'. My reaction was she must be his second wife or something like that. When I approached him he said to the man, he was talking to "This is one of my wife's sons," I was not her son or his son. Then who was I? Now I understand.

Jason was crying; he was holding his face in his hands. "I too have a long buried incident. It was so hurtful that I put it out of my mind. Like you, it was still there. It was at one of the parties; I was bringing up drinks, Avis and the other women she was with were three sheets to the wind. They insisted on refills. As I walked away, one of them ask her, "How on earth did you manage to have a baby? I thought you were fixed."

She replied, "Darling, anything is possible once you know how. Just do not ask my secret. I know, I always said I would never have any brats in my life. When the price is right, you change your mind. Believe me the price was right. My husband is very clever. He knew just what to do. We were running out of funds. Having two babies was a sure fire way to keep us in the life style we love."

Jason said, "At first I thought it was the liquor talking, but she really sounded as though she meant what she said. I felt angry; my two boys were not brats. That woman had to be drunker than I realized. I could not believe any mother would say the things she said. I thought I had buried that incident; but it is still there, clear as the day I first heard it. Now that we have both exposed our hurt, we can forget it."

Pat said, "I had better be getting back to the office. I do not want to go through this again with Matt. Not this soon at any rate."

Jason agreed, "He will be returning soon from his talks with Alan Wilson, I mean Uncle Alan. It is about time you two got to know your extended families."

Chapter 7
EMMA TELLS ALL

Matt waved to his brother Pat as they passed on the drive, thinking, if only I had not stopped to see the new horses when I dropped Mr. Wilson off. He headed for the garage. Jason's car was nowhere in sight.

"Oh well, I will have to wait for him to come home to find out what Pat wanted with him and Cook."

He patted the brief case sitting on the seat beside him thinking Mr. Wilson really does trust me. I could never go in and take the journals without his knowledge. He pondered if he should tell Jason and Pat right away what transpired at the Mausoleum. No, they can just wait a little longer. I want to get started reading as soon as I can. Alan Wilson had won his love and respect.

Matt entered the house through the kitchen. There was Cook with her wonderful cookies. The aroma drifted through his nostrils. He had not eaten lunch. Cook asked him if he was hungry. What a question, he said yes and reached for a cookie.

She slapped his hand and said, "Not yet, I will bring you one of my favorite Corned Beef sandwiches."

"Where is Jason? I did not see his car. Did he leave with Pat?"

"Jason's car is at the service station. He has something to tell you (after he composes himself).

Matt settled in a comfortable chair in his Den and started to read. There was a slight knock on the door and Jason poked his head in, bringing the sandwich on a tray with cookies and a tall glass of ice tea.

"I did not realize how hungry I was until I smelled those cookies."

Jason said, "If you need any help understanding that Journal just ask me. Let me remind you, when I was a young lad he was my Papa too. By the way, I hope you do not mind, I entered your computer notes in the proper sequence. I hope that will save you some time."

"Jason, are you really that familiar with the computer?"

"You are such a young upstart! While you and your brother were away at college, I taught classes at the local High School; I did keep my teaching certification up to date."

"Jason, Cook said you have something to tell me, does it have something to do with what Pat wanted to see you both about."

"That woman, when will she learn to let me decide what to say and when to say it? Yes, it has to do with Pat's visit to Mr. McDonald. I do not wish to get into it right now. I would not know where to start.

Emma entered the room, sat down next to Matt and said, "Well I know where to start.

It has to do with those people that claimed to be your parents.

Jason tried unsuccessfully to quite her. She refused to be silent. Matt was surprised, first at her sitting down in the den, something he had never seen her do; and speaking over Jason's wishes. She began; I will tell you all what Pat had to say. Now just be still and listen carefully." She repeated the whole story adding a few embellishments of her own.

When she finished, Matt clapped his hands. "Who was Mary Wilson? Was she one of the Wilson's relatives?"

"No she was not, my darling boy. She was Nanny." She left us when she got married. You and Pat were at her wedding. She went to live in Michigan with her husband. She has two of the most darling twin girls."

"Matt and I wondered what happened to Nanny. We received birthday cards, from Mary Wilson Kelly, with small gifts. I never knew her name, just as we did not know your name Emma. Do you ever hear from her?"

"Yes, she comes to visit me when she is in town to see her family. It usually is when you are both busy or in school. She keeps your pictures; her girls think they have two older bothers. She will be coming to town in another week to celebrate her mother's birthday."

"Please invite her and her whole family over for dinner. I will tell Pat. I am sure he will be glad to see Nanny again. I do not mean a formal dinner party. Just a family affair, perhaps out in the garden."

Jason asked Emma, "Do you remember how she would introduce the boys to strangers? She would say this is Matt Wilson and the other is Pat Wilson, I am Mary Wilson. She loved the looks on their faces, thinking she was the mother."

Emma chuckled and said, "You bet I remember she was beaming whenever she talked about the adventures with the boys."

Matt told them both, "Mr. Wilson asked me how I felt about our parents, this very afternoon. I told him I considered the names Jason and father to be one and the same."

Again, Jason began to cry. This time Matt put his arms around him.

Jason said, "Emma you should have waited, he has so much to learn from his Uncle Alan."

Matt looked at them both and said, "I never knew Cook's name was Emma. When I heard you telling Mr. oh, I mean Uncle Alan that Pat was going to talk to you and Emma; I did not know to whom you were referring. I feel it is an honor to call you Mother, Emma. You have been like a mother to both Pat and me as long as I can remember. I am glad we do not have to put up with those parties of Avis and George any longer. Jason, do you remember the time when that country was in an upheaval and they took Pat and me with them? They said they were taking us to the Embassy Party and wanted to show us off. I bet it was only to get Mr. McDonald to pay for the trip. We did not spend any time with them. We were stranded in our hotel room; alone and scared. They attended the party without us. We heard gunshots outside of the hotel. I think they would have taken off and left us there by ourselves. Then you showed up. Before we realized what was happening, we were on a private Jet heading for home with you. You turned the trip into an exciting adventure."

"We heard of the problems in that country. Jason replied, Max got in touch with friends of his and discovered you boys were all alone. Papa sent me to bring you back in the company Jet. I had no idea where Avis and George where."

"Uncle Alan wants me to read Papa Wilson's Journal tonight but with all this news I do not think I will be able to concentrate."

Emma put her arm around him and said, "Take a nap and after dinner you will be fine. Now off with you, Jason has plans for tonight. You can read that journal before you see Mr. Wilson tomorrow."

"Jason, you will never cease to amaze me. Are you staying with Uncle Alan tonight? Boy does that feel good to call him Uncle."

Jason told him, "Do as Emma said and get some rest."

Chapter 8
PAPA'S SURPRISE PARTY

As Matt turned to go to his room, he said to Jason, "Uncle Alan told me that he was going to be attending some party with the family."

"True, but he does not know who the party is for. He made us promise not to throw a party on his 90th birthday. That was two weeks age. We made plans to hold it tomorrow. He thinks it is an anniversary party for someone in the family.

Whenever he watched a movie or newsreel of a wealthy or royal family attending a formal dinner he would make fun of the servants standing behind each diner. They never cracked a smile or said a word. They looked stiff and stuffy in their clothing.

Well we have reservations at a private restaurant. The waiters are to be dressed as Robots. There will be one standing behind each of us wearing a gold mask. The Head Waiter assured us that they would be moving in stiff robotic motion. It should be quite a surprise for him. Perhaps he will forget to be angry with us.

John is picking us up tomorrow and driving us to the city. It should be quite enjoyable. All my cousins will be there. We will spend the night at John's house and then I will drive Uncle Alan back here in his car. He can drive in the country, but we prefer he not drive on the faster highways. He has plenty of driving he can do here between the Park and the Stables. I do not enjoy driving in the fast lanes myself.

I am sure he will tell you all about it when you meet with him tomorrow. Do not expect it to be an early meeting. We will all be rather tired.

Before you start reading the journal, let me give you a bait of information. You will notice the title is 'Edmond Wilson's Memories' Author Louise Ryan, assisted by Frank Ryan. Louise was Papa's right arm for so many years; she knew his style and his habits. She also knew that when he finished, he would destroy the tapes and shred her typed pages; if he did not succeed in regaining the memory of those lost 24 hours. Louise knew the real reason for getting him to reminisce was just to keep him away from the office until Dan and I could discover what caused him to suffer such a shock."

Matt asked him. "How did she manage to keep the tapes?"

"She has her ways; she would never lie to him, although she knew Grandma Annie would give her permission to hedge the truth if it meant helping Papa. Papa knew there were two tapes that came with the recorder. What he did not know was that she, Louise, had a brand new recorder in her office. He knew he was using those same two tapes repeatedly. They were old tapes and had Max's name on them. She copied the tape before giving it back to him.

Well, you had better do as Emma said; you can tell me what you think of our ancestors tomorrow. Then I will give you my version of the party; it may be different than Uncle Alan's."

Jason left the room and Matt picked up the journal. Before he could read, the title there was Emma, with her hands on her hips. "Well, young man?"

He tried it again after his nap. He noticed Louise started with the first introduction.

After reading a few pages, he wondered why there were two introductions. Well I guess I will find that out when I read them, he thought.

Chapter 9
THE INTRODUCTIONS OF LOUISE RYAN AND GRACE RYAN

Matt began to read the first introduction of the two lengthy introductions.

Alan asked me if Frank and I would keep Edmond from returning to the office for three or more days. Alan wanted to pick up Dan at the airport. He wanted to retrieve the papers that Edmond had in his hands when he collapsed. Alan wanted to avoid a relapse. For Edmond to lose 24 hours of his memory was not something to dismiss with a grain of salt. He is such a vibrant, active man for is age.

We told Alan we would do everything possible. I said I would talk to his doctor and ask about taking him home with us. With the doctor's o.k. Frank and I went into Edmond's room. We told him our idea to get his memory jolted. He was to be going to our house; and get out of the hospital.

He and Annie had spent many a night in our home and we in theirs. They had their own private quarters at our house, as did we in theirs.

Frank handed me a record and told me to put the extra tape into my purse. When I saw the name printed on the tape, I chuckled. "So this is where the recorder came from. I remembered when Annie and I gave it to Max for his birthday. He was so thrilled.

I am surprised he has kept it all these years. We discovered him taping our private conversations concerning one woman we both disliked. Annie, even with that bright red hair of hers, rarely lost her temper. That day sparks flew from her blue eyes. She grabbed the recorder and went to the open window, pretending to throw it out. Max lunged for the machine and almost went out the window. There was Annie and I holding onto Max's pants with all our strength. We managed to pull him back. Annie made him promise never to tape us again. Later, every time we thought of the sight we laughed.

As I said, Annie rarely lost control of her temper but when she did, it was due to some injustice. I remember the time she really lost it when she heard one of her trusted lawyers was doing something dishonest.

One of the secretaries came to her and told of overhearing Philip talking to one of his clients on the phone. She had been working late and was using a voice-activated recorder. She dropped the papers she was working on. She carefully picked them up after bending down. After going in PHILIP went to REGIE'S desk and began using Reggie's phone. She knew Reggie had been accused of using his phone to make sex calls. Of course, he denied this but the calls were on his phone bill statements. She did not want Philip to know she was there so she kept quite. She remained down on the floor where he could not see her. She discovered later that her recorder was still in operation. She was hesitant in telling Annie that her trusted lawyer was a scoundrel. Annie agreed to hear her out. What was on that recorder astounded Annie. She kept repeating but he is one of the most cooperative persons I know. He is willing to take on any job assigned to him. He is so polite.

Louise said when she heard the recorder it shocked her also. He was telling his client not to worry; even though his wife had enough evidence to convict him of brutality they would drag the case on until the statue of limitation ran out. Philip assured him that the Judge was in the palm of his hand and would cooperate.

Annie said they could not use the recorder for evidence but would put Max on the case to get the evidence they needed to get rid of that bastard. Of course, that meant the judge too. You know Max when he gets riled up he gets the job done. Of course, Max had the charges against Reggie for using the phone for sex calls cleared. Max knew just how to take care of those bastards.

Matt turned the page and said, "what the hell, is this the end of introduction # 1? This next one is by Grace Ryan. I believe she is another one of Jason's cousins. He had better have a good explanation. When is the real story going to get started? I had better read this one and hope here is not another one. No wonder it is so long, everyone wants to get their two cents in."

Matt read the text.

Uncle Alan asked me to retype the pages of Papa's story. Except for the introduction, the original one that Grandma Louise type was ruined. He found it in the strong box Grandpa Frank had left him. The box contained quite a few tapes. Grandpa Frank had his own recorder turned on, unknown to Louise or Papa Wilson. Grandpa Frank had a voice-activated one hidden in his pocket. While Papa spoke into Max's recorder, Grandpa Frank recorded also. Every time he felt, he needed to change a tape he would make excuses to go to the little boy's room. Grandpa kept the tapes in a strong box and gave them to Uncle Alan after Grandma passed away.

Uncle Alan said I should leave out their conversations at bridge and so forth, but that would mean leaving out Anton. I have known him since I was a little girl. He is part of my life. I will do the best I can. I know if I do leave everyone but Papa out there will be a much shorter story.

Perhaps I can do it both ways then Uncle Alan and I will both be happy.

Chapter 10
PAPA'S RECOLLECTIONS
(GRACIE'S" LONGER VERSION)

"I feel foolish doing this Edmond" told Louise, "How do I get started?"

She reminded him that the doctors thought this would help get his memory loss restored. "Just start with the very first thing you remember when you were a child. We are going to talk to you doctor and see if Frank and I can take you home with us. It will be easier for you not being in such a sterile place. We have a nice sun porch where it will be more comfortable and you can have bit of privacy. You record and I will type whatever comes out. No one need know what you have to say other than you, Frank and I. In between, we can relax; have a pleasant meal and a game of Bridge. For that matter, I do not care if you tear up the whole thing when you finish. The main idea is to jog your memory."

"I do not see how it will help for me to go that far back in time, Edmond said. What could that possibly have to do with the missing 24 hours?"

"Louise said, I remember someone telling me of a student that suddenly started to cry in class when a particular subject was being discussed. It turned out the subject triggered a memory of an incident that happed to him when he was very young. At the time, the incident went over his head. He was too young to understand the meaning. In class as on older child, the subject became clear and he now understood the first incident.

Perhaps that is what the doctor was getting at when he said it would help to go far back in your memory. You may find out just what caused your shock. You think about that and when we get home, we will start there with your earliest memories. It will put you in the mood to talk if nothing else. Will you try it for me? Please, while we wait for Frank to arrange to take you home with us?

Edmond said, "This may be boring but if it will make you happy, I will try." He spoke into the microphone. "My very first recollection is sitting at the dinner table with my parents. They were Investment Brokers and owned their own business. The very same one I still operate. At the table, they included me in all of their conversations. When they wanted to ask a question of the other, they always directed the question to me. They did the same with the answers. I loved the attention. It was like a child learning a second language.

Aunt HELEN (Mother's guardian) often told everyone that would listen, my first words were not 'Momma or Dada, they were Stocks, Bonds, and Porfo'. My dad started me on my own personal Portfolio when I was five years old. By the time, I was seven I was a regular Genius at least that is what everyone called me.

My parents took me to the office with them every day. They had a nursery made up in one of the offices. A sitter took care of me while my parents worked. The employees treated me as if I were one of their own. They even talked shop to me.

Aunt Helen was my mother's Guardian when she was growing up. Uncle HENRY, Aunt Helen's husband, ran a large Law Firm that he owned. The Law Firm was adjacent to the Investment Firm. There was an entrance doorway separating the two businesses. When I entered school, the Sitter would take me to school from the Firm and return me to my Parents at the Firm after school. I spent the first ten years of my life in this atmosphere.

Then everything changed. My parents were on a business trip and lost their lives in an accident. I went to live with Aunt Helen and Uncle Henry. Aunt Helen was very upset at losing my mother; the child of her departed sister. She began to smother me with excessive attention. Uncle Henry took me to the office as often as he could so I did stay in touch with my friends at the Investment Firm.

On several nights, I overheard Aunt Helen and Uncle Henry arguing. He said it was not healthy the way she hovered over me. She was so afraid that she would lose me the way she lost my mom and dad.

Uncle Henry discussed his feelings with an old friend of my parents. His name was WALTER BROOKS. He no longer worked with the Firm; instead, he went back to teaching. Walter suggested that I might be happier attending the school where he taught. I could keep my interest up to date in the investment field with him as my mentor.

It took a great deal of persuasion by Uncle Henry. He told Aunt Helen she could pick me up every Friday after school and bring me back to school on Monday mornings. He finally won out. I enrolled at the school the next term. It was a boarding school for boys only. Eventually she began to realize it was best for me to be with my peers. The only time I could go home was on the holidays.

* * *

There was a knock at the door and in stepped Frank, "Hi Buddy, he yelled, get your things together. We are taking you home with us. You can continue your story later"

Edmond Wilson was please to be going to their house. He remembered he had spent many a night at their home with his beloved wife, Annie. This would be he first time he would be there with out her since she passed away.

Sitting in the sun porch he remarked, he felt her presence. They all agreed they too could feel her presence. After breakfast, Frank set up the recorder. "Do you mind if I act like an interviewer, he asked."

"Not at all, Edmond replied, maybe it will help me to get back on track and do what we hope to accomplish. Louise said she would let us 'boys' get on and that she would start typing yesterday's pages. She reminded me that I stopped with the boarding school."

Frank asked, "When did you first meet Charlie?"

"Aunt Helen and Charlie's grandfather JOHN FARGO and his uncle JAKE are first cousins. They lived on a ranch in Arizona; it was a Dude Ranch. John and Jake had no part in running the place. It was just home base for both of them. They loved the atmosphere. Jake was an anthropologist. John was famous in his own right for his photography. John's son JASPER and his wife EMILY were also photographers. They left Charlie with his grandfather to go on a second honeymoon and were lost at sea. Charlie was just a toddler. His grandfather became his guardian. He and Uncle Jake raised him. The housekeeper JODY was like a mother to him. She was also a Fargo, a niece of John and Jake.

Charlie and I are the same age. We met when my parents, Aunt Helen and Uncle Henry flew out to console them on their loss. Charlie and I had a great time. We were too young to understand what had happened. After that, either Aunt Helen or my parents went there at least once a year and I anticipated playing with Charlie.

Uncle Henry was Grandpa John's Law adviser; my parents had been his Investment Consultants. So when Grandpa John came in to sign paper or check things out, he brought Charlie with him in his private plane I guess you could say we knew one another our entire life.

I remember as if it were yesterday, it was the last day of my spring break and Uncle Henry brought me to the office to say goodbye to all my friends. When Charlie and Grandpa John walked in, I screamed and so did Charlie. Uncle Henry had discussed my school with Grandpa John and Uncle Jake.

On a daily basis, on the Ranch, there was no kids Charlie's age to play with. Sometimes the tourist had kids; but they were not there long enough for Charlie to get to know them very well.

His school was far from the ranch. He did not get to see his classmates after school as normal kids do. He was growing up with adults. Grandpa John and Uncle Jake decided to let him try out my school. The next day Charlie was able to see my school. He met Mr. Banks and the other teachers. I introduced him to all the friends I had met. Charlie and I received the same dorm assignment.

Grandpa John said he had a hell of a time convincing Jody to let Charlie go off to school. He had to promise her that she would have both of us every summer vacation. Charlie and I loved Jody.

The school had classes in anthropology for the higher grades. Since Charlie knew so much from his years with Uncle Jake, he was able to sit in on the upper classes. It was not long before they discovered that Charlie knew as much, if not more, than the other students did. Uncle Jake came down a few times to lecture the class. One time he invited them to go on a nearby dig. I chose not to join them. I preferred to stay with Mr. Banks and discuss investments. (Looking back, I wish I had gone with them. Then perhaps I would understand Charlie's obsession with Anthropology).

The summers at the Ranch were gone in a flash of an eye. Listening to Uncle Jake and Grandpa John tease each other about their fields of interest, was enjoyable. I remember Uncle Jake telling Grandpa John that his interest in the camera was just so he could take pictures of animal's genitals. With his face glowing red, Grandpa John replied, "At least I do not bust my knuckles in the dirt like you, crawling around on your hands and knees."

We went with the two of them on a trip to see a beautiful rock formation with the Geology crew. The men were up on top of the rock; Grandpa took out his camera. As he began to shoot pictures, Uncle Jake yelled down, "Do you want us to remove our pants." The men up top laughed so hard we were afraid they would fall off.

We were to do chores at the Ranch with the Ranch Hands while we were there. In return, they taught us how to handle the animals as well as rope acts and trick riding. When we became teenagers, we were able to entertain the guest. The nights around the campfire, telling stories, singing and playing the guitar, all ended much too soon.

I must be getting old, how could I forget the last day at the Ranch? We were feeling rather sad at going home for the last time, knowing that we would be too busy with school to vacation at the Ranch for a few years.

Charlie and I decided to go for one last ride on the two old horses that the guest did not use.

The Ranch Hands treated them like royalty. Grandpa John and Uncle Jake never told us why. We just took it for granted that it was because of their age. We asked permission to ride Mike and Jasper.

When we started out late afternoon Joe called out to us as we were leaving. "Watch out with those old fellows, they have minds of their own."

We were so busy talking about going to college and all that had happened on the Ranch that summer, neither of us noticed it was turning dark. We had no idea where we were. The horses had been following a path up the mountain. We did not know how to get back to the Ranch. Those two old fellows seemed to know the way so we just rode on.

Suddenly there was a large opening in front of us. We saw a well-kept barn attached to a beautiful log cabin. The horses went up to and into the barn. To our surprise two of the stalls had names on them Mike and Jasper.

A light came on and we saw an old man standing in the door leading into the Log Cabin.

"Well, boys you sure took your time getting here. Matty got me on the radio and asked me to keep an eye out for you. Mikey and Jasper were heading in this direction. I am Teddy, a retied ranch Hand. Mikey and Jasper are old timers just like me.

The boys from the Ranch keep me supplied with everything I need. They take turns coming up here for their vacations after the guest go home. Jake and John Fargo said you two could stay the night. We have a private fishing stream. I will take you there tomorrow. Matty will send some of the boys to fetch you back. Mikey and Jasper will be staying here for a while.

Charlie and I wished we had met him sooner. He really had some great stories to tell us that night.

Before we knew it we were graduating and onto college. Charlie added Geology to his studies. I on the other hand studied anything pertaining to Law. Uncle Henry insisted I would inherit his business; he wanted me at least to understand the people working for me. Therefore, I went reluctantly into law.

After college, Charlie went on expeditions with Uncle Jake.

The more I think of it, I do wish I paid more attention to Charlie's love for Archaeology.

I think I would have dropped out of school after the first term if I had not met Annie. She was fantastic. Annie's encouragement helped me to continue with becoming a Lawyer.

We married in our final years. This pleased both Aunt Helen and Uncle Henry; they were happy to have Annie in the family.

After graduation and passing the Bar, we moved in with them in their large house. Annie went to work for Uncle Henry, which left me free to work for the Investment Firm. I did not start as the owner, but at the bottom of the ladder. Most of the old employees were still there and treated me as one of their own.

Charlie had made it back to be my Best Man. Although we saw little of each other, he and I kept in touch. He wrote and so did I. We also kept the phone lines busy.

I remember the day Charlie called to tell me he had met the most beautiful girl in the world. He was working in a small town in Italy on a project, which did not pan out. He was there to close out the project.

The next I heard was that they had gotten married. They were on their way back home. She had a baby (not Charlie's). He apologized for not letting us know all that had transpired but promised to explain everything when we were together.

Annie was pregnant with our Robert and could not make the trip to the Ranch. She insisted I go by myself. I knew she would be safe. Uncle Henry drove her to work every day. She was like a daughter to him and Aunt Helen.

It was good to see Charlie he was beaming with happiness. I was impressed with VERONICA. Charlie was right she was beautiful. Her hair was jet black and her eyes matched her hair. It did not take me long to know that Uncle Jake and Jody had misgivings about her. Grandpa John had passed on of natural causes the year before and Jody still took care of Uncle Jake. Veronica seemed to make a point of never leaving me alone with Uncle Jake. Jody took care of that situation. She had the Ranch Hands take Charlie and Veronica on a tour of the Ranch. Veronica kept insisting that I join them. I begged off saying I was waiting for a call from Annie.

Veronica had a run in with Jody over taking care of the baby. I did not like the way she talked down to Jody. She treated her as if she were a servant. I could see the hurt in Jody's eyes. I put my arms around Jody and kissed her on the check, saying "Do not worry Mom; I will take care of her. The love Charlie felt for Veronica blinded him. He could not see anything wrong in the way she acted.

Uncle Jake wanted me to have complete charge of everything Charlie would inherit. We both knew Charlie had no interest in investments. I tried to explain that Charlie was not the spend thrift Uncle Jake thought. Charlie was not a fool as to where money was a concern. He was just not interested in investments. Just the same, Uncle Jake said he wanted me in charge of a Trust Fund for Charlie. I knew he was thinking that he wanted to be sure that Veronica could not get her hands on the family assets. I said I would agree to do this with Charlie's approval.

Since Charlie and I found it difficult finding time to be alone, he said he would tell me as soon as I returned home how they all met and how everything happened. He did whisper to me in confidence that Veronica hated everything about the ranch. She wanted to live near a BIG city. I told him I would contact a Real Estate Agent I knew of in Midtown. I called Annie and told her that Charlie was interested in living near the city. I asked her to talk to the BAILEYS and see if they had anything for sale on the market in Midtown.

She called me back in a matter of hours. There was a large estate house in Midtown. Annie said the house had a strange history. She and Aunt Helen had seen the property on another occasion. Louise was with them. They all had fallen in love with the location. I told her I did not want her to do too much in her condition. She reminded me that she was only six months along. Aunt Helen and Louise were both there to help. She explained that the house had a large Ball Room where all of Uncle Jake's and Uncle Charlie's artifacts and collections could be set up. It would be a nice place to display Grandpa John's pictures. Aunt Helen took a liking to the Library.

All agreed grandpa's books would go well in there. (Jake had built a storage building behind their ranch house to store the overflow of their collections). She also told me the price was dirt-cheap and some pretty-odd characters have owned it in the past. People thought the house was spooky. Of course, she said, we do not believe in that sort of thing. Some mobsters originally built it. They used it for gambling. Then someone tried to turn it into a school, but that did not work. The latest owners ran a restaurant of sorts. However, that too failed. There were rumors that it was a house of ill repute. Now the house is up for grabs. It is a very well built place. If they do not like it, they can sell it later. At least we will have Charlie nearby. Let us know when we can get started on getting the place fixed up.

I relayed the information on the house to Uncle Jake. He said if Helen gave her approval then it was the place for Charlie. He then said to have Aunt Helen and the girls fix the place up however they wanted.

***

Louise interrupted Edmond and Frank, "I hope I am not intruding. You two are really getting into this story. I would like to add my two cents. I went to see the house with Aunt Helen and Annie. We really enjoyed ourselves. Annie and I were confident we could take care of the Nursery and the Nurse's room. The master bedroom was some thing we did not want to tackle. Aunt Helen called her Interior Decorator MONIQUE to ask her opinion. Monique said she would not handle the job without knowing Veronica. It was decided that Monique should fly to the ranch and get to know her."

Edmond said, "Yes, I was at the ranch when Monique arrived. Veronica took a liking to her immediately. They spent hours talking. Charlie and I were able to spend time together. We went riding on our favorite horses.

When I returned home, I was amazed at what you girls accomplished in such a short time. Louise, what were the three of you laughing about, none of you would tell me?"

"O.K., we were laughing about what Monique had to say concerning her opinion of Veronica.

She told us, Veronica was two persons in one body. One was a Harlot, the other a Pollyanna. We asked her how she was going to do up the Master suite. Her answer was she would make half the room a Harem Sacrum and the other half chintz and ruffles. We told her that would not do for Charlie. She hinted that it would be no time before Veronica managed to have separate bedrooms. She said that in Veronica's mind, she pictured herself as an Aristocrat.

The bedroom was done up in a significant style. For Veronica's clothes, it had a full-length mirror and a large walk in closet.

Annie arranged to have an old friend of ours accept the job of housekeeper. That way we could keep our eyes and ears open to what Veronica planned. SARA had been a housekeeper for a large hotel chain. She was excellent for the position. Her brother-in-law was in the landscaping business. We hired him to work on the grounds. You know the rest. We asked Sara not to let on that we knew one another. We did not want Veronica to know we were meddling in her affairs. We were thinking of how you said she treated Jody. Well enough of that, you two have been talking all day. It is time to eat and have some fun. ANTON said he would join us in a game of Bridge. Turn off the recorder.

***

The next morning, after breakfast, Frank turned the recorder back on. He looked at Edmond and said, "That was like old times last night. Did you enjoy it as much as I did?"

"Enjoy it, I thought a few times Annie was kicking me under the table. Anton plays much the same as I do. Can we have more of the same tonight? A few more days like this and I will have to go on a diet, something I have never done in my entire life. Where did I leave off? Oh, yes, I returned home and was amazed to see how large the place was. I completed the sale.

It only took a week for Charlie and Veronica to settle in. Veronica insisted on calling the place, 'The Manor House'. We went along with her wishes (to us it was still an estate house).

Charlie and I did get to spend some time together. His story amazed me but I did not let him know my true feelings."

"You have sparked my interest. How did Charlie meet this dream girl of his?"

"He told me there had been rumors of an old grave site near a hill in a small town in Italy. His men had been working there for weeks with nothing to show but the bones of a few bodies. He flew out in the family plane to stop the project. Upon arriving, he saw Veronica. She had been keeping the records for the crew chief. The Chief informed Charlie that a scoundrel had deserted Veronica. She thought their wedding was by a priest in Rome. It turned out to be his cousin, not a priest. She was pregnant at the time and ran off ending up in this small town; befriended by a local woman.

Veronica an American was working to get enough money for airfare. She wanted to return to America with her child. Her passport was still good but she needed to have her child added. Without a marriage license, this was going to be difficult. The woman who had befriended her, wanted to keep the child. The woman offered to pay Veronica to return home, but leave the child with her. Veronica refused to do that.

Charlie said they started just being friendly. One thing led to another and before he realized it, he was madly in love with her. She needed a marriage license so he got her one. He married her.

What should have been one week to close the project took three weeks. Charlie had the gravesite investigated. They discovered the names of the deceased. They were relatives to a

BONATELI family living in a nearby town. Charlie arranged to have the bodies brought to the local cemetery. This took more time than he had planned. It also gave him time to be with Veronica. He said he never in his life met anyone as beautiful as she was. She was so charming, and so grateful for everything that he and his crew did for her.

After they married, they went to have the child added to their passports, changing the baby's name to Fargo. When asked for the child's birth certificate, Veronica fumbled around in her oversized bag. The fellow was impatient and asked the child's name. Veronica said Vic.

They returned to the campsite. Veronica borrowed the Chief's car and returned within the hour with the child. Charlie said she convinced him that they had to leave before the woman who looked after the child and her family caused trouble. On the plane, she changed the child's clothing and said, "Do you not just love VICTORIA?"

He called home from the plane and told Jody they were coming to the ranch. Charlie looked at me and said, "You know the rest."

I wanted to yell, I know very little, but kept my thoughts to myself. Once they settled in the 'Manor House' I, thought things would return to normal. Boy! Was I wrong!

Getting alone with Charlie was not easy. Being that the stable connects to the back of the property and since Veronica did not like horses, we decided we would use that.

He told her he wanted to adopt the child. She was afraid an investigation would inform the father of the child's location.

Then in addition, the family that wanted to keep her might cause trouble. She wanted to leave well enough alone. Veronica told him she must have left the child's birth certificate in Italy when they got the passport changed. Her relatives up north said they were going to Italy and would get a replacement. That was the first Charlie heard of her relatives. She told him her family had disowned her when she married (or thought she married) TONY. She did have a few friends that she could count on not to tell her family of her where about.

After Annie gave birth to our son ROBERT, I did not have time to think of Charlie's life style. Aunt Helen became ill and we lost her a month after Robert's birth. We were consoled that she had the chance to hold him. Uncle Henry had one of the offices turned into a nursery. The sitter took care of him in the nursery so Annie could return to work. I worked in the adjoining building, making it very convenient. A home away from home you might say. I am sure Uncle Henry got the idea from when I was an infant.

Charlie and I received word that Uncle Jake was ill. He was getting on in years and wanted to see his boys. Veronica did not want to go to the ranch. Annie wanted to go but we talked her into staying with Uncle Henry. He still had not gotten over the loss of Aunt Helen. On the way to the ranch, Charlie told me that Veronica wanted him to resume his expeditions. She did not want to go along with him. She said he would only be gone for short periods. Then she would try to reconcile with her family. He asked my opinion. I told him it would be good for the child to get to know her relatives.

Uncle Jake and Jody were happy to see Charlie and me. It had been quite some time since we had been to the ranch. There have been a few changes made. MATTY (the ranch foreman) and his family moved in with Uncle Jake and Jody to help her care for Uncle Jake. They helped her with the chores. Once Uncle Jake laid eyes on us, he perked up. The doctor said we were the best medicine he could have.

I called Annie to let her know Uncle Jake was going to be fine. She was overjoyed to get the news and said she would tell Uncle Henry. She insisted we stay there a week longer than we had intended. I was not prepared to hear the rest of her news. She and Louise went to see Veronica at the Manor only to discover that as soon as Charlie left, she got in her car and went up north. Annie said, SARA told her, it was not the first time and she never takes her daughter along. Sara had a phone number that she was to call as soon as Charlie said he would return.

Annie and Louise had little Bobby with them and wanted VICKY to see him. The nurse said, "Mrs. Fargo did not want the child to play with anyone. In fact, Mrs. Fargo never refers to Vicky other than the child. She never has time for Vicky. We, the staff, all want to help the littler girl but know that if Mrs. Fargo hears of it she will let us go and hire her own help. I really do think she resents the fact that you hired us. We tried to let her know we never saw either of you until our interview. I do not think she bought it. What can we do to help, with out jeopardizing our employment? We can not let her know we have been friends for many years."

Annie told her they would work things out. In the meantime, they wanted to see Vicky. She told the nurse if Mrs. Fargo said anything to her she is to tell her that it was out of her control and she should speak to us.

I told Annie I would tell Charlie that Veronica and Vicky were fine and not to worry about staying on longer.

Before the next guest arrived at the ranch, Charlie and I were back in the swing of performing rope tricks and all the fancy trick riding we did as teenagers. We even slept in the Bunk House.

Uncle Jake said he wanted to have a long talk with me about Veronica. He said he had already talked to Charlie. He told Uncle Jake that he became suspicious when his wife started pumping him about his assets. He said he loves Veronica dearly but he is not blind. He informed her that Uncle Jake has complete control over the family business. He added that most of the money goes to Jody, the ranch hand and Matty as well as his interest in Anthropology. He assured her he would have enough to provide her with a comfortable living. That is if they do not overspend.

I cannot begin to tell what a relief it was to hear that. Then I told Uncle Jake of Annie's conversation. He was very cleaver putting the assets in a Trust Fund. We stayed at the ranch a good two weeks. I really missed my Annie and our son Bobby. Uncle Jake made me promise to bring them to the ranch as soon as the weather permitted.

I talked to his doctor and we decided since he made such a remarkable recovery, we would bring him and Jody back home with us. I told Jody and Uncle Jake they would be staying at Uncle Henry's house. It was large enough to accommodate all of us. Charlie said he would offer the Manor House but he knew they would not feel comfortable with Veronica. They started packing right away.

Uncle Henry met us at the airport. They enjoyed their stay but after two months, Jody and Uncle Jake were lonesome for their friends at the ranch. After many hugs and kisses, we took them home. Annie and I both promised we would bring Uncle Henry and Bobby out to see them soon.

Charlie did go on expeditions in the state. As expected, Veronica hopped in the car and went up north. When she received her call that her husband was returning, she came home. She told Charlie she had good news for him. She found the child's birth certificate among her belongs. She suddenly remembered, she was so enraged with Tony, she told the people at the hospital the baby's father was a rapist. She also told them she did not know his name. No wonder her relatives could find no record of the child's birth. The best news of all was that she was pregnant. Veronica told Charlie, "Now you will have your very own daughter."

Annie saw the look on Vicky's face and shouted, "Now Veronica, you will have two children. Maybe this will be a brother for Vicky." Annie asked Vicky if she wanted a sister or a brother. Vicky turned and ran from the room. Annie went after her to console her. She told Vicky what fun it would be to have someone to play with every day. She reminded her of the fun she had when Bobby visited.

Veronica insisted she was going to have a girl and her name would be Charlene. I asked, "Don't you think it would be nice to let Vicky have a say in naming her sister?" Before she could reply, Charlie said it was a good idea. He added, every one would suggest a name for the new baby. If looks really could kill, the look I got from Veronica would have done me in right-then-and-there.

Things went smoothly for the next few months, at least where Annie and I were concerned. I cannot say the same for Charlie. Veronica was constantly complaining of being ill.

At five months, she decided she could no longer sleep in the same bed with Charlie. She used one of the larger guest rooms and had all of her things brought in there. She gave strict orders that no one was to disturb her. That went for Charlie too.

Plans for an exciting expedition for South America were underway. They asked Charlie to help set it up. He declined the offer due to Veronica's condition. She would have no part of him staying home just for her. She said he made her uncomfortable, never leaving her alone long enough to get the rest she needed. She was seven months and said he would only be gone one month.

The housekeeper, Sara, told Annie that as soon as his car left, Veronica was in hers and heading north again. Before the month was up she was back home with a beautiful baby girl. Veronica said she had no time to notify anyone. It all happened so fast. The nurse that accompanied them took the baby up to the nursery. Veronica went straight to her room to rest. Charlie lost no time in getting home. One look at that beautiful little bundle and he was lost in shear excitement. He was amazed at how much she looked like the baby picture of his mother that Uncle Jake kept on his dresser.

Charlie said he would like to name the baby EMILY. That was his mother's name. Veronica did not object. She knew Uncle Jake would be pleased to have the baby named after his beloved niece. (Uncle Jake did have control of the family assets).

***

Louise entered the room, "Well my dear boys, time to call it quits for now. Anton has made us a light dinner and he also promised to be a forth at bridge again". She changed the tape in the recorder and followed them out of the room

Edmond asked, "Just how long has it been that Anton worked for you?"

They both laughed, "Anton is an author and has never worked for us. He came to live with us as a houseguest. That was before our Gracie was born. You must remember when our daughter was date raped at college! He stayed on to help us try to find the bastard that injured her. Our KAREN was never the same after the baby was born. Anton did his best to convince her it was not her fault."

"Yes I do remember Annie and Max tried every method they could come up with, but to no avail. Anyway, it is best that you never found him. Annie, you, Louise, Max and Anton would most likely be spending your life in prison and Frank and I would spend time visiting you."

"After Karen past away, Louise said, Anton stayed on to console us and help raise Gracie. He is still here, now a member of the family. Oh! He still keeps up with his writing. Frank and I would be lost without him.

You boys can start again recording tomorrow, after good nights sleep.

***

The next morning, after setting up the recorder Frank said. "Lets see if we can find those missing 24 hours."

"Frank, do you remember where I left off on this memory hunt of mine?"

"Yes, you were at Emily's appearance and Charlie's delight."

"As I recall, the next fifteen years seemed to fly by; Charlie kept going on his expeditions and Veronica went up north (without the children). Uncle Henry was semi-retired and my brilliant Annie ran the Law Firm.

Veronica came down with a fatal illness. Charlie was distraught. I went to the Manor to check on Charlie. He was coming out of Veronica's room looking white as a ghost. My first thought was she had passed away. Before I could utter a word, he motioned for me to follow him to the library. After we entered that massive room, he went to one of the sofas and sat down; putting his head in his hands and cried. I do not ever remember seeing him in such a state of despair. He blurted out. "I do not know who that woman is; certainly not the one I loved. For a woman who is dying she looked upon me with contempt and hatred in her dark eyes. She wanted me to know what really happened when she met me."

She told me, "The Chief told me that you were coming to shut down the project. He also told me how wealthy your family was. Immediately, I made up my mind to trap you into marriage. I was an actress and knew my trade well. There never was a Tony or a child. I used them in my scenario to get your attention. My beauty was my asset. You and your chief were so gullible. I had enough money of my own to return to the States if I choose. I was there on a vacation. I knew of a family with too many children. They just had a set of twins. I did not like the man, he was nasty to me and his wife did not like me either. I stashed away baby supplies, waiting to get you in my grasp. After we married, I used the chief's car to pick up one of the babies. I left a larger sum of money for the father; counting on his greed not to look for me. I thought he would blame his wife for losing one of the babies."

Charlie could not bear to enter her room again, even after she did pass away. He left the girls with the nurse and took a long trip trying to clear his head and heart. He was able to lose himself in his work. When he returned, I asked him what his plans were for Vicky. Would he try to find her parents and return her to her rightful family? His answer surprised me.

"No, no, no if I do that I could be convicted of kidnapping. At any rate, the girl has been my daughter all these years. She is Emily's sister. How could I send her back to a life she has never known? I cannot punish her for what Veronica did.

At times, she has a nasty streak in her. I credit that to the way Veronica treated her. I will continue to be her father."

Then he caught me off guard by saying he was preparing to give me his complete Power of Attorney. He planned to go on more expeditions and wanted to know if I would take care of all expenses on the Manor and anything else the girls needed.

He and I both knew I could never take advantage of my friend of so many years. He said I would receive the customary fees for the extra work. He would have it no other way.

Then I received that dreaded call from Matty at the ranch. Jody was too upset to call. The doctors gave Uncle Jake a month or two to live. Jody wanted us to come right away. I contacted Charlie and we arranged to go to the ranch. Uncle Jake perked up as soon as he saw us. It was apparent that he did not have much time left. He made me Executor of his Will and handed me his Power of Attorney for the time being. Charlie was in complete agreement.

***

Frank asked, "Do you smell something cooking? I bet Anton is here. I will check with Louise."

She said, "Anton has out done himself with this dinner, we are going to have a guest or two so turn off that machine and get ready for a fun evening."

***

The next morning as usual Frank set up the recorder and said, "Do you realize this is the fifth day we have been doing this?"

"Five days? I did not think it has been that long. I guess when you are enjoying yourself time really does fly. Louise, did you hear from Alan or Dan?"

"Yes, they went to the office to see what was in the papers Eve said you were holding when you collapsed. They think they may have found Charlie's location. They have gone to the Manor and arranged to have every thing put in order for Charlie's return. I understand from Eve that they flew to Italy. She said they would call when they have results.

"Well that is a relief. I wonder if he is looking up Vicky's family to ease his mind. Did he do the right thing in not telling her of her birthright?" Do you remember where I left off on this story of mine?"

Uncle Jake had just made you his Executor and gave you his Power of Attorney."

"Yes, I remember now. Charlie and I stayed with Uncle Jake until he told us to get lost. He did not want us hovering over him. Jody did that and it was all he could take. We went riding but not with much enthusiasm.

I dreaded making the call to Annie. She said she would get the children together and fly down. Vicky and Robert were already in college. Emily was graduating and ready to join Vicky in the fall. When they arrived, Uncle Jake was surprised at how much they had grown. Vicky was a tall slender girl with long brown hair and brown eyes not at all like Veronicas. Emily had long red hair. Her beautiful blue eyes seemed to shine with a radiance that filled the room. Robert looked more like Annie than me. He even had her interest in the law.

Uncle Jake passed away in his sleep that night. After the funeral, I asked Jody to return with us. She said her home was with Matty and his family, especially with the new baby. Losing Uncle Jake was painful for all of us. Jody did stay on with Matty and his family. We did not tell her what transpired with Veronica."

***

There was a knock on the door, this time it was Anton. We told him we had just started and to give us more time. He showed us the tickets he had for a game we wanted to see. We were delighted with that news and decided to continue tomorrow.

***

With the children away at school, Charlie resumed his love for the excitement of finding new discoveries. He received word from Sara saying Vicky was throwing wild parties at the Manor. He came home to find that Sara was right. He found thirty or more college kids roaming through out the house. They even managed to ransack the old wine cellar down in the sub basement. They were drinking and doing things that made Charlie extremely angry. He was relieved to find that Emily was not among them. She had transferred schools to start her study of Geology. She wanted to surprise her father and join him on his trips. Vicky promised him she would never bring her friends to the Manor again. She said, not all of them had been invited. He was disappointed with Vicky. She had no interest in college other than to have a good time. She said she would change school and try her hand at acting.

The next year Emily called her father and told him she planned to marry HARRY BURNS, a fellow student in her Geology class. Charlie came home to meet this fellow. Harry was on his best behavior and met with Charlie's approval. I think Vicky was furious, at least that is what Annie and Louise told me. They thought Vicky wanted to be the first one to get married and to make Charlie a grandfather.

Louise and Annie saw to it that Emily's wedding was beautiful. Vicky played some pranks but in spite of her all went well.

Within a year Emily, announce she was expecting a child. Vicky did a completed turn about and helped her sister. Harry disappeared a month before the baby was due. No one could find him. We hired the best investigators but to no avail.

Vicky announced at the time she too was expecting. She thought Harry was the father. She said she did not want Emily to find out.

The nursery was equipped and a nurse hired to help care for Emily. Emily was distraught over Harry's disappearance and her health seemed to be going down hill. The baby was born, a little boy. She named him Daniel. Charlie was elated to have a grandson.

Vicky had taken another trip to New York, as usual. Emily thought Vicky had heard from Harry but she returned with no news. She said she hired her own investigator and he told her he had some leads but it would be months before he knew anything concrete.

Emily's health had improved to the point that Charlie felt it would be all right to rejoin his men. Vicky also left for a trip back to New York. She told Emily she could have some good news for a change.

The nurse told us Vicky returned late one night and asked her if she would go to the kitchen and fix up a light snack; she was exhausted from her trip and had not eaten all day. She was starting to show her pregnancy. When the nurse returned with the food, Vicky said the baby was fast asleep. She asked the nurse to join her in the other room and told her she dreaded telling her sister that her husband may have been involved in some sort of crime. He may be the one the police are looking for.

Frank asked Edmond how he knew all of this. He replied, "If Louise would come in she could answer that question, it was Louise and my Annie that told me everything that Sara reported to them."

"How come I did not know of this?"

"You were too busy keeping the office running smooth for Annie. You really were a workaholic. We were lucky to get you to play Bridge with us."

"I heard that often enough from the girls."

To continue, the next day the nurse asked her if she heard anything new. Vicky assured her that she would inform her immediately if her contact called. The nurse went to care for the baby and was startled to discover that the baby had gained so much weight. Vicky said she would have the doctor over to check on Emily. She was worried that her sister was getting weaker by the day. She was lifeless and sleeping most of the time. The following morning the nurse went to ask Emily a question and could not wake her. She had passed away during the night.

It took a long time for all of us to get over the shock. The nurse confided in Annie her concerns about the baby gaining so much weight over night. She said some how he did not look like the same baby. Yet he was not out of her sight for any length of time. She thought she might have imagined it with her worry over Emily's health.

Vicky was now getting larger and larger. She told Charlie that she was going to drop out of school to take care of both babies. I am not sure he ever heard her. He wanted to rejoin his crew. It was the only place he could forget his grief. Annie and I were reluctant in his going to something that could be dangerous in his state of mind. Nonetheless, he insisted in going. He asked me to keep close watch on his grandson. Of course, Annie and I planned to do just that.

About two months later Vicky told the nurse she was going to New York to get a progress report on Harry. She did not want him to just show up and claim Daniel. She told the nurse she was taking a companion with her, so not for us to worry.

"Louise, I bet you remember how surprise you and Annie were when she returned with her son."

"Surprised? Indeed! We both said just like Veronica, some coincidence. She named her baby VINEE. We wondered where that name came from. We asked her but she would not answer. Victor would have been a nice name but Vinee is just a nickname."

"Charlie came home to see his grandsons on a regular basis every three months or so. Burying himself in his work was the only way he could cope. He asked me again to take good care of them while he was gone. He always called in advance to let Vicky know he was coming, so she would not be gone somewhere with the children. He was unaware that she did not take the children anywhere ever.

***

"Well, Frank said, it is time to change the tape again. What do you think about calling it quits for today? Are you up for more Bridge after dinner? Anton is looking foreword to continuing yesterday's game where we left off."

***

After another nice breakfast, Edmond continues, "Sara the housekeeper called Annie to tell her she was going to quite her job with Vicky. She told Annie, "I am getting too old for this. I went through a rough time with Veronica; I can see it happening again. That woman does not spend time with either baby. Perhaps that is good for them. She completely ignores little Daniel. It is as if he does not exist in her eyes."

Annie asked her to stay until she could get someone trustworthy for the children's sake. Sara told her there was a local girl she thought was perfect, Annie knew her. The name was MOLLY RILEY. Annie did know of her family. Sara agreed to stay on and train Molly. Her training will include all of what she is required of her and what was not required of her on the job. Molly was delighted to have a position in the Manor. Molly was too young to assume Sara's duties. However, would fill in where anything to do with Vicky was concerned. She helped the nurse care for Daniel. Molly brought Daniel to the kitchen area every day. Everyone took turns playing with him. They loved him and he loved them in return.

When Vicky discovered Molly with Daniel, she gave her permission to keep him down there with the staff. For a nursery, they will fix up a room near the kitchen. Molly had been at the Manor three months before Vicky even noticed her. The only instructions Vicky gave Molly were, when Charlie came home, she was to bring the child to the upstairs nursery. Vicky told Molly to stay with Daniel and keep him away from Vinnie. Molly was not to let Daniel play with Vinnie's toys. When Charlie left, she was to bring him back downstairs again.

Protecting him from Vinnie was all anyone really wanted to do. That Vinnie was a monster from the start. One of the staff found a door in their room leading to the third floor. This is a secret from Vicky.

Molly's boy friend, BERT BENSON, built a play area with all the pleasures a little boy could wish for like being equipped with slides and swings. They made Daniel understand that it was a secret. He was not to tell Vicky or Vinnie. He knew this as a way of life. Aunt Vicky and Vinnie were mean to him and he did not want them in his domain.

I was grateful that we had Sara (she decided to stay) and NURSE TUDDLE to keep us informed on what is going on at the Manor House. Molly could not bear to leave little Daniel. Bert understood he was very fond of the little tyke.

Annie asked me if I could arrange for Bert to live at the Manor. I said I could give him a part time job. That way he could keep his business in town and still be with Molly and Daniel. I paid him his wages in room and board plus a modest salary. I also matched Molly's wages to that of Vinnie's nurse.

Bert spent many hours with little Daniel. When Annie brought our grandson Alan out to the Manor, Bert would take them both to the stable to ride ponies. Alan loved to play in the secret playroom on the third floor. Just outside the window, there was a large flat roof. Bert made a nice porch for the staff. They held picnics on that roof. Vicky never discovered their secret.

Our Max asked Annie if she wanted him to follow Vicky up north to see where she spent so much of her time. Annie would have no part of that. She said leave well enough alone. We really do not care as long as she leaves us time to ourselves.

I guess all things do come-to-an-end. Vicky somehow discovered that Bert and Molly were married (nine years) and made life miserable for Molly.

She complained constantly, and tried to get me to fire Molly. I of course refused. I told Charlie what Vicky was up to when he came home for his visit. He decided to have Daniel's name changed to Fargo. He said it grated on his nerves that Vinnie was a Fargo just because his mother was not married.

He had Annie look into the legal ways to get this done. On Daniel's tenth birthday, he became a Fargo. I asked Charlie if it would be possible for Daniel to go to school with Alan. My son Robert and his wife Susan would love to have both boys stay with them. Daniel moved into Alan's room with him.

Vicky went on a rampage when she heard the news. She had Charlie so upset he came over to my house and we talked for hours. He went back to the Manor and left that night leaving a note telling me that he will call as soon as he is settled.

***

Louise interrupted for super and a game of Bridge. She said, "I think you have done enough recording of your history. It has not done any good as far as finding those missing hours. My granddaughter Gracie asked me if we could plan a trip to the ranch while we are still young enough to travel. Eve said you have not had a vacation in years. It would do all of us good go have a break. Gracie will make the plans. Everything is running well at the office. By the time, we return so will Dan and Alan. I hope with news of Charlie.

***

Matt closed the folder containing the journal pages. He said aloud, "This is the strangest journal I have ever read." He picked up the intercom to call Jason just as Jason entered the Den. "Jason you are just the one I want to see. How can anyone call this a journal of Edmond Wilson's life? It includes Louise

and Frank's activities in the conversations;" "I can explain
that, Louise knew Papa would delete the tapes and shred all
the typed pages. She wanted Dan and Alan to hear his story
in his own voice. Reading something on paper is not the same
as listening to the sounds of the human voice. Papa did indeed
erase the tapes and he did shed all her typed pages. She did not
let on to him how disappointed she was. She still had her own
tapes. As it turned out, Frank used his own voice-activated
recorder unbeknown to either Papa or Louise. He put the secret
tapes in a safe place for Dan and Alan.

Years passed and Uncle Alan had Gracie transcribe them.
She was a court recorder and typed them verbatim. You would
not expect her to leave her grandmother or grandfather out of
the reports. Although I suspect she also added some of her own
recollections. Do you understand the sort of person our Papa was?"

"Yes indeed, though I never met him, I know by this journal
he was a loving man. Did you know Gracie well?"

"She was family, Papa was her Godfather, and I was a
friend of her husband. I was the one that introduced them."

Matt said," He never finished the journal."

"There was no need to, I am sure Uncle Alan will give you
the details at your next meeting. Now off to bed with you, it
is late. I am going to spend the night at the Manor with Uncle
Alan. Do not expect to see him too early. We had quite an
exciting evening"

Mat asked, "Do you think it would be a better idea for him
to come and stay with us here? Emma would not mind, I am
sure. I'll ask him tonight."

Chapter 11
THE PAPERS

The next morning Matt headed to the Manor House. He held on to Papa's Journal tightly. (As if it would jump, right out of his hand and fly back to the secret drawer in the Pillar). Using his personal key, he entered the Library. Locking the door behind him, he went to the back of the room and opened the secret panel in the bookcase. He then carefully went down the stair and into the Mausoleum.

Alan Wilson was sitting in one of the large overstuffed chairs reading a book. He looked up at Matt and said, "I see you have finished the Papa's Journal."

Matt replied, "I asked Jason why it was not finished and he said to ask you."

"In due time my young friend". Alan put down the book he was reading and continued, "I have read this book each year since it was published. I find it a retreat from daily life. This book takes me away from all my cares and worries. I feel refreshed and able to face what life hands me with renewed strength. Now tell me what you think of our Papa Wilson after reading his memories."

"Well Sir, even though I never met him, I respect what I learned not only from the journal but Jason and yourself. He must indeed have been a very special person. Jason tells me that Louise and Frank's granddaughter, Gracie, transcribe the journal from the tapes you had. I was confused when I kept reading Louise and Frank's accounts in the journal. It took me all-day and late into the night before I finished. Is Gracie still around? Was she part of the Foundation? Do you trust her not to reveal what was in the journal? It could be mighty tempting, for someone to get that information"

"Not Gracie, she loves Papa too. I do not think she really read what she typed. She was more interested in my personal typewriter. Eve gave the darn thing to her when the work was finished and bought me a newer model. I did not type often enough to need a newer one. I guess it was more for Eve than for me. Something Eve planned on doing and did not get around to it until then."

Matt asked him, "Were you surprised at your party last night?"

"Yes indeed, my family really pulled a fast one on me. Did Jason tell you about it? Until last night, I thought I could read Jason like a book. He and my boys went to a lot of trouble arranging that affair.

Now I want you to meet the rest of the Original Members. They were all my best friends. In this place, they are still very much alive to me. Of course, you can only read the report that explains how they felt about Vinnie and his mother Vicky. First, I will explain how we came to meet and join in this partnership. Each one has their own personal view of Papa.

I believe I told you that I picked Dan up at the small airport where we kept our company Jet. On the drive to the office, he filled me in on what he discovered during his trip to California. The strange incidents, that puzzled him. Now let's get on with my telling you about the things that happened to bring about this whole setting."

***

Dan and I went straight to the office to look at those damn papers Papa was holding when he had his attack or whatever it was that made him collapse.

My lovely wife Eve was in the office gathering the papers off Papa's desk and putting them in his Brief Case. I scolded her for not going straight home as she said she would. She said Papa wanted his keys and she told him she had given them to me at hospital. She knew I would want the keys when I returned with Dan from the airport. She promised Papa she would go to Louise and Frank's house and return the keys.

I told her "I do not have the keys. You have them. Why did you tell him I had the keys? "

She replied, "Because I knew you and Dan wanted to see the papers in Charlie's private cabinet. You could not do that without the keys. Take the papers out and lock the cabinet. Then I will return the keys to Papa. I cannot drive with the medication the nurse gave me. Max is going to take me there and then drive me home."

Dan asked her if she felt up to letting us know exactly what transpired prier to Papa's collapse. She said, "It seems impossible that everything that happened was just early this morning." Then she told us that Papa was so exuberant when he arrived from his trip to the Manor House. He must have gotten up at the crack of dawn. He met the locksmith and had him change the locks. Vinnie had changed them when his mother died. He would not let Papa enter the Manor. That made Papa angry, as he was the one in charge of managing the place for Charlie. We knew how nasty Vinnie could be. Papa argued with him for over a month. Vinnie had run off all the staff. The house and the grounds were in dire need of tending.

Eve continued, "Papa had this big brief case with him. It held all the papers he colleted from Vicky's desk. He was anxious to find information concerning Charlie's where about. He had not heard from Charlie since Vicky died. He seemed so pleased with himself as he poured the papers on top of his desk. I went about my business when suddenly I heard him call out, No. No. No. and he got up and headed toward the file cabinet. The one he keeps Charlie's papers in. He opened the drawer and just stood there. He was holding a stack of papers in his hand. I went over to him and saw he was staring straight ahead. I put my hand in front of his eyes and he did not move. I tried to remove the papers from his hand. His grip was so tight it crushed them together. I pulled as hard as I could while trying to get the papers from his hand.

He folded like an accordion. I was standing there with the papers in my hand and screaming. The next thing I remember was the ambulance people putting him on the stretcher.

Dan asked if he could see the papers Papa was holding. I went toward the file cabinet with Papa's keys. I heard Eve gasp. I said to her, "Sweetheart, I am not going to go through the files. I know better than that. We just want the papers he was holding in his hand when he fainted."

Papa had explained to both Dan and me that the file was his private property. He told us both it obtained his Power of Attorney from Uncle Jake and His authorization from Charlie, for all expenditures on the Manor and the girl's welfare. He kept every letter Charlie wrote. In the letters, he asked him to send large sums of money. Papa said, without those letters he had no proof Charlie received the money. Papa did not want anyone to think he spent the money on himself. As it was, everything the girls needed Papa would send his own money. That was money from his own pocket, not reimbursed by Charlie.

I opened the cabinet and there they were, sitting on top of the pile. They were from Charlie to Jody, Uncle Jake, Matty and several to Papa. We stuffed them into the Brief Case intending to look at them later. I really did not want Eve to see what was in them to cause Papa such a shock; at least not until we read them ourselves. I knew my beloved Eve could not keep a secret from Papa. I told her she should leave and go to Louise's house and give Papa his keys. At the hospital, they gave her strong sedatives and I could see she was still under the influence. Then I reminded her she promised me she would go straight home.

Dan and I told her we were going out to the Manor House to see the condition of the place. It had been more than three months since Vicky died. Vinnie had fired the whole staff including the gardeners. She wanted us to wait until the next day. We said the sooner the better. The new key was on Papa's desk. The front door was the only one with a new key. We did promise her we would a least stop somewhere to eat.

The drive to the Manor seemed longer than usual. We were both in a somber mood for some unexplainable reason. When we arrived, we found a note from PAUL, the locksmith.

He wrote he would change the rest of the locks the next day. He also wrote that he contacted MIKE MAHONEY to arrange for the cleaning people and the gardener to come and fix up the place. Mike had done all the carpenter work at the Manor after Bert retired. Everyone agreed to come over and get to work. There was a lot of work we needed to do.

We entered the Library and opened the Brief Case putting the papers on the long reading table in the middle of the room. Dan and I looked at the letters first. Under them was another set of papers. It took a while for us to realize what we were looking at. On the paper, Charlie's signature, written over and over and over. To say we were shocked is putting it mildly. Someone was copying his writing style. The pages of all his words repeated until they looked like his. Dan said, "Remember what Max taught us, look at the fact with our eyes not our emotions."

That was easier to say than to do. It was too over whelming. We had to get our thoughts together. We put the papers back into the case. If this is what Papa saw, no wonder, he was opening Charlie's file cabinet.

Dan said, "Look at the dates on these letters. Was Charlie's wife Veronica still living then? Maybe she was the one forging Charlie's signature. Perhaps she wrote herself checks or signed sales slips or something like that. We will have to check to see who was around at that time period. We do know Charlie was still around when he adopted me. These pages of his hand writing might have nothing to do with Papa after all." We decided to have a look around the Manor.

Chapter 12
A NOSTALGIC TRIP

The old playroom was still there; with all the toys, we enjoyed so much when we were young. We went to see what we could find. Bert had sealed the upstairs door. We remembered another way to enter through the large pantry.

At the back wall of the pantry, Dan reached down and pulled a lever under the shelf. It was much lower than he remembered. The cased of canned goods turned, revealing a hidden staircase. He put on the light switch. "Well, looks like it still works he said. I do not remember the staircase being so narrow. I guess when you are small everything looks larger."

We went up to the third floor, where our toys had been (hopefully wishing they were still there. We opened the door and to our surprise everything was there, covered with sheets. Molly must have done that before she moved out. We removed the sheets and looked with wonder at what was our playground. We saw the two large hobbyhorses that Bert had made for us. Dan said, "Remember the times we pretended we were cowboys on these very same horses? We will have to take them to your house and watch your boys have fun games on them just as we did."

"I told him, they had their own horses. Papa had Bert make smaller ones for them. These horses would be too big for them. Do not forget my boys are 3 and 4 years old."

Dan looked surprise, he said. "I do not remember Bert making horses for the boys."

"Of course not, they were delivered the week before Bert was killed in that accident at the theater; when his scaffold broke. You were distraught. Bert was always like a father to you. We both considered him your fairy godfather and Molly your fairy godmother.

When you came to live with my parents and me, they still came over and took us places. It was months before you were able to accept his death. Dan agreed that was a rough time for him. He turned toward the back wall wiping his eyes.

I asked, "Do you remember that place in the wall where food was brought up from the kitchen. It was for our picnics. I think they called it a silent butler or something like that. Look over here. It is the patio door. I wonder if the furniture is still there. Let's look outside; no, the patio is bare."

We looked out at the landscape only to discover that some one had put up a large fence blocking the way to the stables. We both knew who did that. We decided to have it torn down.

We went back inside and went to the room next to the playroom. It was a very large room with a basketball hoop at one end. On the floor was a yellow line painted. We were never to cross that line. The room below that side of the floor was the Library. We were not to make noise on that side or Vicky might hear us.

We decided we had enough time to relax and went back downstairs. We left the kitchen and headed toward the Library. Dan stopped and looked at the oversized pot holding a scrawny dead tree. He said, "Something will have to be done with this poor thing. I remember it as having a thick green bush. I used to hide behind it whenever I heard Vinnie or Vicky coming I was not to be in this part of the house when they were around. Molly was afraid if Vicky found me in her part of the house, she would fire Molly. I remember one time I almost got caught. This is when I hid behind that large green bush. I think I was about 7 years old.

One day Molly took me upstairs and showed me how to escape if Vicky came home and I was upstairs. Do you want to see the escape route I had to take?

I asked him, why I never knew of this before? We played in the foyer when I came to visit. Although I do remember hiding from that, mean Vinnie.

Dan said, "Vicky would never get away with hollering at you. Your parents would not allow it and they knew it. Come, follow me and I will show you the way. We went up stairs. Then Dan said we have to go to the far end of this hall. There is a sitting room with an open door. Molly said I was to open the closet and go inside. She pulled this lever. Watch, the back wall turns in. There is just enough room to squeeze through. When I was young it was easy, but we are much bigger. Molly said I was to wait for her to come and help me down the stairs. Do you recognize this landing? Up those stairs is the door to our playroom" I said to Dan, we must have misunderstood Bert when he said we were never to cross that yellow line because the Library is below. The room under our playroom is the sitting room.

"Did you ever use the escape plan?" Matt asked

"No, Sara had someone working outside when I played in the forbidden part of the house. After having a very close call, they would signal when Vicky's car approached."

I will tell you about that incident. Vicky and Vinnie were at some luncheon and I guess Vinnie got into trouble. I was playing in the foyer when suddenly I heard her car. She almost drove it into the house. Vinnie was screaming his heads off. She had him by the ear and dragged him into the house. She told him to get straight upstairs and not stop in his playroom. I was hiding behind the planter. He stamped his feet up the stairs. Molly and Sara came running from the kitchen. Vicky told them to mind their own business. Vicky had her back to me and I waved to Molly to let her know I was safe. Vicky went to the Library and shut the door. I was going to run to the kitchen when I heard Vinnie coming down. He was crying," Mommy, please, I am sorry for spilling the food. That waiter bumped into me. I could not help it Mommy. Please do not be mad at me, I love you Mommy." Vicky came out of the Library and he put his arms around her, hugging, and kissing her hand. She forgave him of course; and called for Sara to bring some dinner upstairs for her little angel. I could see Sara glancing in my direction.

Vicky returned to the Library but this time she did not close the door all the way. There was a small opening. I was afraid that if I ran out from behind the bush she might reappear. I waited for the longest time and decided to sneak a peek through the crack in the open door. I did not see her anywhere. I got brave (or dumb) and opened the door wide. Then I went inside to see if she had fallen behind her desk. She was not in the Library. I knew she did not go past me. There is small alcove at this end. I thought maybe she was in there, I looked; I guess my curiosity got the better of me. She was not in there either. It is a small area. I knocked over a small statue that was on the shelf. I bent down to pick it up. When I straighten up, I saw Vicky standing behind her desk. Then my courage disappeared. I did not want her to find me and fire Molly. I crouched as low as I could. She headed in my direction then turned and went to the door and left. I waited for a while and then I went to the door but I could not open it I was scared. The next thing I knew, Molly was opening the door. She grabbed me by the arm and we ran as fast as we could to the kitchen. Everyone was so happy that I escaped without Vicky catching me. They all took turns hugging me. Bert came rushing in and asked me if I wanted to go to the stables with him. He was finishing a job for them. Of course, I was very happy to go. I loved that man like a father. Until now, I put that incident out of my mind. We are telling Papa to try to remember things in his past and we are doing it ourselves.

As we entered the Library Dan said "Look around and see for yourself. There is no way I could not have seen her. She was a tall woman. Come to the area and see where I was crouching when she reappeared. I know what I saw."

I said to him, "You say she was standing behind her desk. Let's go see if there is another secret door back there."

We tapped on the paneled wall behind the desk and it did not sound hollow. We looked for a switch or button, anything that would reveal a secret door. The back panel had a recessed case built in that held figurines. We picked up each one of the figures hoping to find a switch. There was nothing below or behind any of them. We then searched the desk; looking for a clue, still nothing. I hit the side of the case in anger and the bookcase on the left side moved back and turned inward. Dan wanted to go in and see where the passage led. First, we closed it and tried to open it again. It worked, but we wanted to be sure when the door shut we would be able to come back out. Dan went in and closed the door while I stayed behind to open it for him. Suddenly the door opened and there was Dan, laughing at me. I guess I looked scared. We again opened it and entered. Vicky must have been taking good care of her secret staircase. It was all clean and all painted white. The staircase to our playroom not being used for fifteen years or more had cobwebs. This one had a long stairwell leading down, deep below. At the bottom to the right was a very heavy wooden door. We opened that one with ease. The other side led into the old wine cellar. We went to the far side of the cellar and discovered that the door had been bolted shut from the inside. I remembered there was a door in the basement that was off limits to us.

The basement had large beautiful white and black tiles. Dan wondered if our old cars were still under the stairs, that lead up to the kitchen. Bert bought those cars for us and took us down to the basement to ride around in them. Since we would have to go back up to the kitchen and find the stairs to the basement, we decided to do that later. We retreated, locking the wine cellar door and bolting it the way it had been. We went to the heavy door on the other side. We tugged hard to get it open. Looking inside we saw a desk and chairs and other furnishings. It looked like a shelter of some sort. A number of shelves loaded with out dated can goods. It must have been a bomb shelter at one time judging from the items on the shelves. We saw two large freezer units, (very old ones), but still working. Vicky had back up electricity installed in the house. It appeared that she did not want the freezer to turn off for some reason.

The room was spotless. I did not think she was capable of doing housework. We opened one of the freezers and had the shock of our lives. For the first time we understood how Papa felt. It contained the body of a young man in his early twenties. A newborn infant lay across his arms. We closed it quickly not wanting to believe what we had just seen.

I looked toward the desk and noticed a diary and a strong box. We took the strong box but left everything as it was and went up the stairs. We staggered up the stairs was more like it. To say we were stunned is putting it mildly. I suggested we should have taken the diary too. Dan said, "I am not going down there again tonight." For safekeeping, we placed the box and all of Papa's papers behind the secret panel. We knew in our hearts that if Papa found out about this it would surely kill him. I suggested we look at those papers again. He reluctantly agreed saying we would do that after we had more time to relax and get our wits together.

There was a knock on the door; it was Mike's wife. She was working to get the kitchen cleaned up. She asked if we would like some refreshments. We were glad to take her up on her offer. In the kitchen someone looked at Dan and said," You look as though you have seen a ghost." I agreed and explained he is suffering from Jet Lag. He just arrived from California this morning and we have been on the go ever since. She offered to make up one of the rooms if he felt he needed a few hours to nap. We thanked her for the offer and said we would like the refreshments now.

We went outside to watch Mike and his men take down the fence that was blocking the road to the stables. Mike told us that when Bert was living here, the town folks would take that road as a short cut to the stables. Otherwise it is a long way into the next town and then turning back to get to the stables. He said he knew the Mrs. would not approve. Therefore, the town folks pretended to be tradesmen. She did not find out until years later. That nasty boy Vinnie told her. That is when she put up this fence. Everyone in town will be happy to see the fence removed.

Chapter 13
BACK TO THE PAPERS

We returned to the Library ready to tackle those damn papers. This time we saw that there were more letters than we had seen originally. We did not know when Charlie wrote them. I said I would call Eve and ask her if she remembers the last time Papa heard from Charlie. Eve told me Charlie had called and left a message two months ago or maybe it was three. I told her we were still trying to find Charlie's location. He travels to many places around the globe. Eve said she was sure Papa had received a letter from him. She was not sure of the date but it was not all that long ago.

We looked through Vicky's desk to see if Papa had missed any letters. Sure enough, he did not remove any letters addressed to Vicky. Several were from someone named VITO in Italy. We read one of Vito's letters to her. From the sound of the letter, he did not like her at all. In the letter we read, he told her not to come to his town and disturb his family again or he would not mail any more letters to Edmond Wilson. He wrote that if she did he would write to Mr. Wilson himself and tell him what she has been having him do. He said he did not like making her deposits. She would have to go to the bank and make her own withdrawals.

We did not like the sound of this. When we began to search for the address of this Vito there was a letter addressed to him from Vicky. It read, Dear Brother of mine, my own twin at that, if I want to see OUR MOTHER, I will do just that. Now do as I say or you will regret the day we were born. The envelope had his address on it. The date on the letter was two weeks before she died. We were glad Vinnie did not get his hands on it. We found nothing else that was useful.

So, Vicky had a twin brother!!!

If Papa suspected the letters from Charlie were forged, both Dan and I agreed that would explain his attack and his missing 24 hours. It would be too much for him to bear. We still did not know where Charlie was or if he was even alive.

I told Dan I would call Louise and tell her not to let Papa remember anything after Charlie adopted Dan. When I called her and told her what we had in mind, she whispered into the phone. "Did you find anything? Is Charlie dead? I told her we did not know but it looks like it. Just keep Papa occupied until we figure this mess out. She agreed to do this. I also told her that Vicky had a twin brother in Italy named Vito. Maybe we can get some information out of him.

Dan said, "We can not handle this by ourselves. We need help. That is when we decided to get in touch with Dan's fiancée, Claudia. We needed her to round up Michael, Richard, Kathy and Margo. We needed people that knew and loved Papa. People we had complete trust in, before we told them of our discovery. Maybe we will find out why some of them were in California when Vinnie had his accident. Dan had discovered this when he went to investigate Vinnie's accident.

I suddenly remembered that I could not meet with them that evening. My boys were in a church play and I promised I would be there. Dan said he would go alone, but I said we were in this together and I wanted to be with him. He was in no shape to go it alone. I called Eve to let her know everything was fine and ask her what time the play started. I was relieved when she told me the play was not until next week. Therefore, we were on for the tonight. Dan and I went out to a restaurant in town. That was more to kill time than to eat. Neither of us was hungry.

At the appointed time, we went to Claudia's house. To our surprise everyone was there waiting for us. One look at us and Claudia knew something very serious had happen. They all agreed that we both looked washed out. We told them Papa was in serious trouble. What we just discovered would destroy his reputation and more than not kill him. We needed to know if we could count on them for help. Each of them had the same response. "HOW?" I said, "First I want to know your opinion of Vicky and her son Vinnie."

Renee spoke up and said she would be very glad to tell us what she though of the bitch and her bastard. Michael agreed to assist her in any way he could.

After Renee's story, we said it was too late to go into anymore. Everyone agreed to meet the next morning at the

Manor House. Dan and I were the only ones that were ever in the house. They were anxious to see the inside, now that Vicky and Vinnie were both dead.

***

"Matt", Alan said, "before I tell you more I want you to read the stories told to Dan and Me."

Alan Wilson went to the pillars and opened the drawer. He took out three journals and handed them to Matt.

"These journals are not as long as Papa's. Read them tonight.

Incidentally, I have decided to take Jason up on the offer he made me to move in. If he really meant it, I am going to accept.

Matt was delighted, he said he would tell Emma right away. He knew both she and Jason would be please.

That night, Matt looked forward to learning about the other members of the Foundation. Jason often referred to them as his Uncles, Aunts and Grandmother. He decided to start reading the one titled Renee and Michael

Chapter 14
RENEE AND MICHAEL

Renee started, "Before I tell you why I was in California I want to clear up the rumor of Vinnie trying to rape me. I was home from college for the summer break. There was a course offered at our High School that fit into my schedule. My Godmother Molly had warned me many times to beware of Vinnie. I did not take her seriously. Every time I met up with him, he was charming.

One evening as I was leaving he said he would walk me to my car. On the way to the parking lot, he grabbed me. His big hands covered my mouth. He dragged me to the rear of the building and forced me to the ground. I was stunned. I remembered the warning Molly gave me too late. I was too terrified to scream. As he tried to remove my clothing, someone hit him hard across the shoulders. It was Bert. He grabbed Vinnie and yelled at him, saying if he ever came near me, again he would kill him. I remember Bert saying, "Your mother will not be able to protect you. You are a monster. "He said much more but I was too scared to remember everything. Bert helped me up and said he would contact my parents.

They wanted to call the police, but Bert said it would not do any good. Vicky had lawyers from up north that would turn things around and make it look like I had been trying to come on to her 'Little Boy'. Bert told my parents that he also had friends. They would scare the Monster into leaving me alone.

I was grateful; the course I took was finished. I could never go back to that school again. I was unable to leave my house for fear I would run into him. I did not want to return to college. My friend, EDNA, lived in California. She came to tell me she would go back to college with me. She promised that if I came with her she would not let me out of her sight. She showed Vinnie's picture to all of the security guards at the college. They guarded me as if I was some kind of royalty.

After graduation, my parents said I could go to California and spend time with Edna and her parents. That is why I was in California when you saw me. The day I was to return home is the day Vinnie had his accident. If I had known he was in California, I would not have gone to meet Edna's parents. They are wonderful people. I would have missed a memorable experience.

Edna had gotten a job in a reality office. I wanted to see her before taking my flight home. As I was about to enter the hall leading to her office a figure brushed past me so forcefully I hit the wall. There was a strong smell of whisky and who knows what else. I did not get a good look at him but a feeling of horror consumed me.

I went to Edna's office. She was out for few minutes and a woman sitting near the door said I should wait at Edna's desk. It was at the far end of the room. As I sat down, I saw a frosted glass door directly behind the desk; I heard a loud voice. Someone was yelling profanities. There was another voice but it was soft and calming. I froze. The vulgar one sounded like the one in my nightmares. When Edna returned, she said the insurance people use that door when they have business in her office. It is a matter of convenience.

We went out to dinner later and heard on her car radio news of Vinnie's death. I would be lying to say I was not relieved. I could not help but wonder had that been him yelling in the next office. For a split second, it occurred to me to tell someone about the incident. It was only a split second and the thought was gone. For the first time in almost two years, I felt free.

MICHAEL said, "When I picked Renee up at the airport I knew there was a change in her. She had been unable to tell me of Vinnie. I knew it bothered her. At last, she told me the whole story. It was a good thing Vinnie was dead or I would have looked him up and finished him off myself.

Michael turned to Alan and said, "You and Dan discovered something that could destroy Papa Wilson. If there is anything at all I can do to prevent that from happening, I am here to help.

When I was looking to refinance my Dance Studio, I found it very difficult. There were repairs I felt needed attention. I was at the Bank still trying when I saw Richard talking to Papa Wilson. They motioned to me to come to the office and join them. Papa said Richard told him of my problem. Papa said, "I hope you will not object but I had our man Max investigate you. I know you have trouble getting a loan. If you charged the full going rate for your students, you would not need a loan. "

I told him I was more interested in teaching the children than charging them more than their parents could afford to pay. Papa said he found that very refreshing in this day and age. Then he told me he was going to give me a Grant. He said I would not need to refinance, just consider it his gift to the arts. I have had numerous meetings with him since. I have become very fond of him. He promised he would dance at our wedding when Renee and I marry. We cannot let anything happen that could hurt him. Let me know what help you need and we will be there.

When we meet at the Manor House tomorrow, will you give us a tour of the place? I have always wondered what the inside was like. It is so large from the outside. We told them all we would be glad to show them the house from the inside. Dan and I had not been there since we were ten years old. We were rediscovering things we had forgotten. For now, we would like to hear from Kathy and Richard; that is if they are willing to confide in us.

Chapter 15
RICHARD AND KATHY

Richard was the first to speak, holding Kathy's hand he began, "I get the feeling that you are more interested in our impression of Edmond Wilson, then in finding out why we were in California. After all Vinnie's death was ruled accidental.

So here goes, my father was Mr. Wilson's personal Banker for many years. I saw him on many occasions while working with my dad. Dad knew he was reaching retirement age and would not be working many years longer. Mr. Wilson was pleased that I am going to handle his accounts, with Dad's guidance of course. Mr. Wilson insisted I call him Papa.

I know personally that everyone that has dealings with him respects him. Have you any idea how many people he has helped or donated money to the needy? Even just, being there to listen to their problems?

As for my being in California, Kathy had a job working for a theater company in that state. She had been helping Claudia and Margo with the small local group here in Midtown. She received a chance to try her hand doing costume designing in California. We all thought, Margo, Claudia and me, that it would be good for her to try something other than just the small group at home. She hesitated but we convinced her to go.

The theater owner and Producer was a fellow named JACK DYLAN. Kathy sent a picture of the theater group to Margo and Claudia with the names attached. Claudia looked at the picture and called me immediately. Claudia said the man in the picture identified as Jack Dylan was really Vinnie Fargo.

I called Kathy and told her I was on my way to California and I will find a replacement to finish her work. When I told her the man was Vinnie Fargo, she said it could not be him. This Jack Dylan was too charming. He never once tried to be anything other than a friend. Although Kathy had never met Vinnie, she heard of his reputation.

When I arrived at her apartment house, she was not there. I went to the theater but found it closed. It was early afternoon. I then went to the tavern next door to inquire about the theater and see if they knew Kathy. The owner (MIKE) said "We are closed if you are looking for someone maybe I can help."

"I am looking for Kathy, the costume designer for the theater."

He said, "She was in earlier that day waiting for a girl that was going to replace her. She had her Portfolio with her and showed me her drawings. She is quite talented. The other girl did not show up. I did not see Kathy leave. Who are you anyway?"

I told him I was Kathy's betrothed. Before I could get another word out, he started yelling at me for allowing a sweet girl like her to work with that scumbag, Jack Dylan. He said I should be ashamed of myself. I told him I was there to take her home. If I had known it was Vinnie Fargo, she would never have been there in the first place. He ask me what I meant by saying Vinnie Fargo, that is Jack Dylan. I told him, Vinnie must have changed his name.

One of the fellows sitting in the rear came up and told us Kathy had received a phone call from the other girl saying her child was ill. She asked Kathy to come to her house and gave an address over the phone. He wrote it down for Kathy in his Sales Book. He showed us the address on the carbon paper in his book. The owner, Mike looked at it; he slammed it down on the table and said we had to go there right away. He said there was no girl living at that address. It is next to his brother's apartment. The only ones in that apartment are a bunch of party guys. Mike said he would call his brother and we could get in through his brother's balcony window.

I went numb. Before I knew what was happening, we were rushing out of the bar. I was in this stranger's car, racing down one street after another. When he stopped the car, his brother, whose name I cannot remember now, was waiting outside.

We went up to his apartment and out onto his balcony. He entered the window and the next thing I knew there was Mike helping Kathy over the railing onto his brother's balcony.

We ran down the back stairs. Mike asked his brother if he would be safe. He replied "Hell no, when Jack finds out his entertainment is gone, it will not be safe for anyone to be around." He said he would go back to the tavern with us.

Kathy spoke up, "Never in my life did I expect things to turn out the way they did. I got to the apartment and rang the bell. Some man answered the door. I thought I had the wrong apartment. Before I could say anything, he grabs me by my arm and I was inside. When I saw all those men, I wanted to run. A man who took my Portfolio stopped me. He looked at me in a strange way and asked, "Are these the acts you will be performing for us today?"

To say I panicked does not half explain the fear that engulfed my body and mind. I looked toward the door next to me and saw Mike peeking through. He motioned to me to come. He looked like an ANGEL. I do not remember much of anything else except for crying so hard in Richard's arms. My nightmare was over."

Richard continued, "Mike and his brother dropped us off at Kathy's apartment after I reassured them I was taking her home. I rented a large Van and we packed her belongs in it. We both needed to eat but decided to wait until we were long gone from that place. We rested for about an hour. I told Kathy I had some papers to drop off for the Bank to a former Insurance Agent from Midtown.

Kathy remained in the car while ran up to Milo's office. Kathy put a covering over her head and wore dark glasses. I told her not to open the door for anyone until I returned.

She pretended to be reading a book. As I handed Milo the papers we heard loud cursing coming from the hall. Milo ran and hid behind a cabinet and motioned for me to be quite. Vinnie staggered in. The room reeked of liquor the moment he entered. He mistook me for one of the insurance agents. He threw a policy down on the desk all the while screaming something like, "She can not do that to me. Take her name of the XXXXX policy right now"

His language was revolting. He staggered out of the office and I shoved the policy in the wastebasket.

Milo said, "He must have met his match. Vinnie's mother had a large paid up policy with her name as beneficiary. I have a feeling he stole it from her. Every few months he comes in and changes the beneficiary. Usually he comes in cheerful and cocky. I wonder who the lucky girl is to be free of him.

I went to his apartment once. There in his private office he had some of the most revolting items I have ever seen or want to see again. He had this enormous rubber like form of a man's penis in full erection. There were others but this one was a shock. He kept a hat on top of this gross thing. I suppose he had pleasure in seeing the faces of the girls when he asks them to hand him his hat."

"We took the policy out of the wastebasket and read it. To my horror, it had Kathy's name on it. I gave Milo a quick explanation of what happened. I said I would call him when I returned home safely with my girl and give him more details.

I hurried downstairs to the Van, which was out of Vinnie's view. We drove for hours before stopping to eat. We heard on the Radio of Vinnie's sudden death.

When we reached Nevada, we decided to stop. After stopping, we decided to get married. Kathy called her mom. She was so angry with me I thought she would hate me for life. When she heard what happened. She was grateful. I saved her sweet girl from a fate worse than death. The marriage was in name only, to save Kathy's reputation driving across country with a man.

When we returned home, I made a call to Milo and told him the whole story. He said that since there was no time to change Vinnie's policy, Kathy would be getting a quarter of a million dollars. Kathy and I both said we wanted no part of that money. Milo said that was foolish since there was no one else to receive it. We could always give it to a charity. Therefore, that is what we plan on doing. We are setting up a Trust Fund for the Community Theater.

Renee heard me screaming at Vince. Incidentally, Alan, my dad and your dad, Robert, were classmates in college."

***

Matt finished reading two of the reports and called Jason. He said, "Jason now you can read them. Did Uncle Alan go off to bed yet?"

"You bet he did, Emma and he spent several hours playing Pinochle. Uncle Alan said he did not care for Bridge like the rest of the family. He and Emma are two happy card players.

I have read Papa's Journal but I never got to see these, my aunts and uncles. You do not know how much this means to me. Uncle Dan let me read Papa's Journal, but he passed away before I had the chance to read the folders. I did not let Uncle Alan know I read the Journal. He was too depressed. He was the only one left of the Original Members of the Foundation.

Matt told him. "It would be better for you to read Margo's story tomorrow. I should be finished reading it by then. This is just too much to absorb."

Jason took the stories of his Aunts and Uncles to his room to read in privacy. "I have loved them very much; now I can understand how they became involved in the Foundation, he said as he entered his room."

Matt decided to finish Margo's story that night. If I do not he thought, I will have Jason breathing down my neck. He settled down in his nice comfortable chair and opened the folder titled 'MARGO'S STORY'.

Chapter 16
MARGO'S STORY

I suppose it is my turn to speak. I know everyone is wondering why I left a good career in New York, to come to a small town like Midtown to work with the community children. This is where I grew up. This is my hometown. I did not leave here by my own choice. Vicky Fargo really kidnapped me. I know I cannot prove it but she did take me away from here.

First, let me tell you of my beginnings. My father was an older gent. He was referred to as, 'Stage Door Johnny'. He got one of the girls in the chorus in trouble, she wanted to get rid of the baby but he would not let her. He paid her a great deal of money to give him the baby.

When I was born, he brought me to his niece and her husband to bring up. He paid them a monthly fee for my support. Their farm was not doing to well at the time and they needed the money. AUNT DORIS told me she would have taken me in without being paid support money. She loved me as her own. UNCLE HERMAN was like a father to me as I was growing up. Aunt Doris smothered me with attention. When my father would come to visit, I thought he was my grandfather. I called him Papa. It was not until my teen years that I learned the truth.

I could not go to my classmates homes. They were always welcome to come over to the farm. We held picnics and parties on the farm. I was immature for my age. Aunt Doris was always the chaperone at the school functions.

When it came time to go to the Graduation Prom, Aunt Doris was ill. She let me attend the Prom without her and was not able to protect me. Sometime during the dance, one of the kids spiked the punch. Bert and I drank it. I do not really remember what happened that night. I later learned I was pregnant.

Aunt Doris blamed herself for not being there for me. I thought she was angry with me. Uncle Herman was so mad he would have killed the boy if he knew who he was. I knew I was with Bert, but to this day, I do not know what happened.

Somehow, Vicky found out about the wild party. (Vinnie was probably the one to spike the punch), she stopped me on the street one day and told me my aunt Doris wanted to get rid of me because of the shame. The church banned my Aunt Doris and Vicky said it was my fault. She said she knew of a place that took care of wayward girls like me. She said she would take me there. I got in her car and she gave me a pill with a glass of water to calm my nerves. The next thing I knew, I was in a strange place. I discovered later, it was in New York. A nurse met us and ushered me into the building. I was frightened and wanted to see my Aunt. Vicky told the nurse that my family wanted nothing to do with me any more.

It was a home for unwed mothers. They were nice people and tried to be friendly. I was keep isolated from the other girls. The doctor and his wife that volunteered their services were very lovely people. They took a special interest in me. Vicky said I could work for my room and board by helping them in their home.

I lived with them until my baby was born. The nurse said the baby died. No one informed the doctor of me having the baby and he was angry. He demanded to see my little boy. They informed him the baby was no longer there. He had been sent away to be buried. DR MILLER and his wife took me to the cemetery to see the grave. During the delivery of my baby, I know I heard him cry. The nurse insisted that the baby was stillborn.

When I wrote to my Aunt Doris and Uncle Herman, I received the letters back stamped with large letters, WRONG ADDRESS. Mrs. Miller wrote to Vicky asking her where my family was. Vicky wrote back saying my aunt died and my uncle sold the farm.

Now I was really homeless. The Millers took me in and cared for me as if I was their own child. I learned to love them. They put me through college. They had a little girl that died when she was just around ten. She would have been about my age.

I loved going to college. That is where I learned acting and producing shows. The Millers were elderly. When they passed away, they had me in their Will giving me everything they owned. I became very wealthy.

As the years went by, I could not stop thinking of my dear Aunt and Uncle, and all the love they had given me. It did not seem right that they could stop loving me so suddenly. I only had Vicky's word for it. I came back to find out for myself what really happened to them. The farm was still there. Uncle Herman still ran the farm. They did not sell it. When he saw me, he cried with joy. He told me Aunt Doris was in a nursing home due to poor health. He was sure that when she knew I was back, she would get well. He said they hired an investigator to find me. Every lead was a dead end. They had a typed note I was supposed to have left. It said I was going to find my mother. There were various signs that I had gone to California. It contained the last known address of the theater where my father met my mother.

I told Uncle Herman I had written a letter to them, but it came back stamped, WRONG ADDRESS. I showed Aunt Doris the letter at the nursing home. She showed me a note she kept all these years. The note was typed. I did not know how to type at that age. Even the signature was typed. She said she never received the letter I wrote. Looking at the date, she said that was when my father passed away and they went to his Funeral.

Vicky Fargo made arrangements for someone to take care of the farm while they were gone. Aunt Doris said she thought Vicky was being too pleasant. She said she never did like that woman. With my disappearance and my father's death, she was not thinking clearly. Aunt Doris told me Mr. Wilson had his own private investigator, Max, try to hunt for me, but to no avail.

I cannot prove that Vicky was the one who kidnapped me. It would be my word against hers. Vicky had some very sharp lawyers. With the Millers gone there was no one to verify my statements.

Aunt Doris and Uncle Herman lived on the farm until recently. Something they talked about when I was young was to move to a retirement home in Florida. Now I have plenty of money and I sent them to one of their choosing. I visit them on a regular basis. This is my hometown and I want to spend the rest of my life here making up for lost time. If that Witch were here, I would make her tell what happened to my baby.

I ran into Molly, my old school chum. She told me that she had worked for the family taking care of Emily's son Daniel. I asked her when Daniel was born. She said his birthday was May 1. Then she told me Vicky also had a son named Vinnie. His birthday is May 25. My son was born May 5.

I remembered seeing Vicky when I went into labor. She was talking to the nurse. Vicky was definitely not pregnant at that time. I began putting two and two together and wondered if Vicky's son could be mine. I began to question Molly about the time Vicky brought her son home. She was not there at the time but told me Sara and the Staff was puzzled. Vicky came home with a private nurse. She would not let any of them see her son, not even the nurse taking care of Daniel. Could it be he was not as old as she said?

Molly told me about her adorable little charge. She also told me how much she and Bert loved him. I knew then that if Bert had been the father of my son, I would never tell them. I could see how much she loved Bert. I did not want her to become suspicious with all my questioning. To change the subject, I asked her about Bert.

Molly wanted me to go with her to the Theater and see Bert. He was rebuilding the upper balcony. We saw Bert standing on his scaffold. He looked down at us and the railing came loose. Bert fell at our feet. He was badly hurt and died a week later. I felt responsible for his fall. I though maybe the shock of seeing me caused him to become careless. We later learned it was a faulty railing.

Molly and I resumed our friendship. She filled me in with her life at the Manor with Bert and little Daniel. We spent many hours discussing Vicky. I kept prodding her for information about Vinee. One day she said that she did not want to hear that name again.

Molly had not been back to the Theater since Bert fell. I convinced her it was time to see the wonderful work he had done for the Theater. We were to meet that afternoon. I said I would be with her. She was upstairs when I arrived. I went up the stairs to the balcony with one of the girls (Nancy).When we reached the top all I saw were two legs going over the railing. The sight seemed to freeze in my mind. I also remembered Bert as he fell.

I was overwhelmed with guilt for talking her into going there. I do not remember leaving the theater. In my high heels, I ran for miles. When I reach the Manor House Gate, I collapsed. Some one picked me up and drove me to the hospital. My feet were bleeding so badly they kept me in the hospital overnight.

I went home in a wheel chair. I was totally incoherent. I kept repeating, "It is all my fault." If I had not come home, they both might still be alive. The doctor assured me that Molly had a Heart attack and was dead before she fell.

The reason I was in California was to see if Vinnie could be my son. When I saw him, I knew there was no way in hell that he could be a child of mine. He was vulgar, a drunken slough. I was on my way home when I heard the news of his accident. I cannot say I was sorry.

As for Papa Wilson, I will be forever grateful for all the assistance he gave to my Aunt Doris and Uncle Herman. They would have given their last dime to find me. He saved their farm. He was very kind to them. I will do anything I can to protect him.

***

The next morning Matt gave the folder containing Margo's story to Jason. Jason told Matt he was taking his Uncle Alan to the city to pick up a change of clothing. They would be back after lunch. Matt would be free to visit his brother Pat, Jason said, "I will call you and let you know what time to meet Uncle Alan and where."

Chapter 17
INSIDE THE MAUSOLEUM

After visiting his brother Pat and filling him in on what had transpired, he decided to check out the Mausoleum while waiting for Alan Wilson to return.

Matt entered the building and walked around looking at the various plaques. He read the names engraved on them. He stopped at Margo's with a deep appreciation for the woman now known to him as Jason's Grandma. He then moved to the one marked Renee and Michael, two lovely people that thought more of giving lessons to the children than making money. On the other side of the room, there was a plaque for Richard and Kathy. Matt's brother now holds the position Richard held for the Foundation for so any years.

He thought of Kathy and Claudia working with Margo to bring culture to the children in the community. There was one for Dan, Alan's lifetime friend.

Now Matt understood how Dan and Alan were able to meet in this place called a Mausoleum. It was really a Memorial to those wonder people. It still did not explain the reason for building the Mausoleum.

"Hi there young fellow, I see you are admiring the Plaques. We had not planned to do that at first. Claudia thought it would be a nice Tribute. Did you read the reports, he asked Matt?"

"Yes, did they know you were going to keep records of their statements or whatever you call them?"

"Of course, Dan asked for their permission. Margo was the one who said, we had better because she would not repeat it again. We felt that they had nothing to hide and were really interested in helping Papa."

Matt looked at Alan Wilson and asked, "Are you alright? You look pale."

Alan replied, "You would think that after all these years I would not feel so emotional at remembering these incidents. I am rather tired. I told Jason to leave me here but; there is so much more I want to tell you."

Matt said, I would call Jason and have him pick you up. You can rest in one of the rooms and continue when you feel up to it. "

Alan thought for a minute and said,"I would like that. I should discuss some things with Jason. Perhaps I will steal him from you and have him take care of me. I am alone in my big house now. I could go live with the children but they would hamper my freedom."

Matt got a big grin on his face. "Would you consider moving in with Jason and me permanently? That way Jason could take care of both of us. You can tell me all I need to know in my den. Also you and Emma can continue playing cards."

Jason was delighted to hear the news. He arranged to have a room made up for his Uncle Alan. After serving them their dinner, he went to Alan's house" to bring all the clothes and items Alan wanted in his new room. On his return he told Alan, he had a talk with his son John. He was happy to hear that his father would be living with Jason and Matt. They had been trying to get him to live with them. They knew his rambunctious grandchildren would drive him crazy. After his nap, he met Matt in the den. He said, "Now I can get started with the rest of the story."

Chapter 18
FRIENDSHIPS

We met with Claudia and the rest of our friends. We felt assured they would help with Papa. We told them what we found, (The Papers and the bodies in the Freezer). We needed their help in deciding what course of action we should take. It was too late to do anything to Vicky or Vinnie (they were both dead). We had to keep Papa from ever finding out what had happened.

We did not know who the young man was. Dan and I had decided not to mention the baby after hearing Margo's story. Then Dan remembered that we did not look in the other Freezer. Michael said, "You promised to give us a tour of the house. We can go and have a look together after the tour. I do not think it would be a good idea for the girls to see the body. We can bring up the diary and look through that strong box. Perhaps we will find a clue that will tell us who he is."

Norman's wife knocked on the door and asked if we wanted to have lunch with them. I was amazed at how far they had gotten on fixing up the kitchen area. Norman's wife, PATTY had ordered a supply of groceries and had them delivered. She and the girls that she brought along helped her fixed a grand meal. Patty was going to set us up in the dining room. We said we preferred to eat in the kitchen with her staff. She liked the sound of 'Her Staff'.

As we were eating, Patty told us Sara had told her about the secret stairway to the third floor. I asked her if she would like to see it. After we ate, Norman opened the entrance that Bert had hidden from Vinnie and Vicky. We took them upstairs to see the picnic area where the staff held their private parties.

Dan asked Norman if his men finished tearing down that damn stockade that locked the path to the stables. He said they were still working on it. We then took the group down to the basement. We showed them the wine cellar. We also showed them under the stairway where our cars were hidden.

Bert had boarded it up. It took no time for us to pull the boards off. There they were our very own cars. We laughed at the size. What seemed so big at the time for ten year olds, were tiny now.

I looked at Patty and could see she was already planning on how to use the third floor picnic porch. She said she would have the secret stairways cleaned up when they finished taking care of the rest of the house.

We returned upstairs and showed them the large pantry. Then we showed them the silent butler and the secret entrance that lead to the sitting room on the second floor. The girls were interested in seeing all the bedrooms, especially Vicky's room.

After the tour Michael, Renee, Kathy, Margo, Richard, Dan and I returned to the Library. We opened the secret bookcase. They looked down at the stairwell. Richard remarked on how clean it looked. It had fresh white paint applied on the walls, ceiling and the stairs. No one would guess what a grisly secret lie down below. "Perhaps it is not as bad as it first seemed to us. There are eight of us to ponder what has to be done." Richard said. We all agreed to bring up the Diary and look in the strong box. Kathy suggested we bring up the Diary and read it before opening the second freezer. Richard asked Dan, just when was the last time he saw his grandfather, Charlie Fargo.

Dan said, "I will have to think on that one. It has been a long time. I do remember him coming over but there was not anything special about his visits. What I remember clearly is when we all went to the Courthouse to change my name to Fargo. Papa and Grandma Annie met us there. After the Judge talked, to me he signed some papers and we all left. We went to dinner to celebrate. Grandpa Charlie and I got in his big car. I forget the driver's name but he was a friendly fellow.

Grandpa and I sat in the back seat. He put his arms around me, kissed the top of my head and told me I was now a Fargo. He said to have it done he adopted me. I was now his little boy. I do remember it was pleasant having him all to my self. He did not get angry when I spilled my desert. It was a chocolate pudding. I thought someone said it was a mouse. I jumped and it spilled but not before, I had eaten some. He took out his handkerchief and wiped my face. He put the dirty handkerchief back in his pocket."

Michael and Kathy volunteered to get the Dairy from the shelter themselves, promising not to open the freezer. When they returned, they both said that it was a very cozy place. They saw the bunk beds and supplies; it was well equipped. Richard said, "What the hell, if we do not go look into the other freezer we will be thinking of it instead of what is in that Diary. Let's us go down and get it over with."

Dan could not bring himself to open the freezer so I did. Just as we suspected there was another body. This one was an older man. Dan took a look and said that is Charlie Fargo. He pulled the handkerchief from the pocket. On it was a dark stain smear. Dan said, "This is the handkerchief that has his name embroidered on it and it is the one he used to wipe my mouth. He told me it was a gift from my mother. She had made it for him. Vicky must have had him murdered that same night. How could she have kept that a secret, all these years, without Papa getting suspicious?"

We hoped the Diary would answer that question.

Chapter 19
READING VICKY'S DIARY

Kathy thumbed through the pages of the book. We all wanted to know how anyone could be capable of such horrible crimes. We wanted to know how her mind worked.

She wrote that her 'mommy' had given her the Diary as a present on Christmas. She states. "With her eminent death it seemed ironic that I should be writing about her. Dear Mommy, what shall I write in a gift you saw fit to give me let me see, what shall I start with? Is Mommy going to die?

When I over heard her fighting with Daddy, I learned for the first time I was not his daughter. I was frightened he might send me away. I ran and hid in the Library. When I heard Daddy and Uncle Edmond coming, I got behind the large desk. Hearing Daddy say he would not send me, back to Italy was such a relief. I decided to be a good daughter. That only lasted until I realized Emily was his daughter, Emily would inherit everything. That is when I decided to get rid of my dear little sister somehow."

Kathy said, "Do I have to continue reading her words? I would rather just tell you what it says in here.

So then, it says Emily married Harry. Harry was a friend of Vicky's; she had her eyes on him first long before Emily even met him.

When they announced they were expecting a baby, Vicky decided she could not let that happen. She called Harry to the Library to tell him of an important discovery she had made. She showed him the secret passage. When he went down the stairs, she used a hammer she had hidden to hit him over the head. He rolled down the stairs and she hit him repeatedly, to make sure he was dead. Getting his body into that freezer was not easy. His blood was on the stairs and the wall. The blood would not wash off. She had to paint the whole thing. It was not a simple task. She gave orders to the Staff never to enter the Library when she was in there. She told them she was working on a surprise for her sister.

Vicky pretended to be pregnant also. She told Charlie that Harry had raped her. Harry's disappearance was a mystery to everyone. Now she had to get herself a baby.

Pretending to be growing larger was no problem. She had the answer to that from her mother when Veronica pretended to be pregnant with Emily. Vicky used the same padding her mother used. Veronica had told Vicky how she managed to fool everyone, including Annie and Louise.

Veronica had a picture of Charlie's mother that she stole from the photo album that Uncle Jake had on his dresser.

Mother called her lover, Pauley and asked him to find a perfect match an unwed mother with the same features as the picture. Then she purchased all those stomach pads. She had hidden them in the secret room behind her closet. When Veronica was dying, she told Vicky of that room. That was where she kept the bankbooks with her name and Vicky's. She told Vicky to use the money for herself in case Charlie stopped supporting her.

Kathy ignored the next lines in the Diary that Vicky wrote. (I heard of a young girl in town that was pregnant and made plans on how to get that baby).

Claudia interrupted, she said, "I think we should stop for now. The Diary has more pages than we have time. We either look in the Strong Box now or call it a night. We can come back tomorrow. We need time to get our thoughts together. Dan and Alan are exhausted". We all agreed with her.

"I remembered that night. Eve was asleep when Dan and I arrived home. Eve had a busy day. I did not want to wake her. Dan and I did not look in on my boys. We knew if we woke them, they would be all over us. We most certainly did not want to wake Max. I crawled in beside my wife thinking, I wish Dan and Claudia would get married so he could feel the same comfort I was feeling. Sleeping that night was more comforting than I could have imagined.

In the morning when I awoke, I found a note on my pillow from Eve; it said she was going to have breakfast with the boys and Max before going to the office. She wrote I was sleeping so soundly; she did not have the heart to wake me. She also wrote that I should call her at the office. Max was due back from taking the children to school around ten or so. I woke Dan, we wanted to leave the house before Max returned.

Tonight we will be getting home earlier and it will be good to lay with the boys. Max caught sight of Dan as we were leaving and asked him if he read the cable he sent concerning Papa. Dan just looked at him and said, "Of course, you gave yourself away in the heading of the message. It should have a family name such as Alan, Max or Eve. Why all those STOP marks?" Dan turned to me and winked. Max, said "O.K. so you got me."

Dan and I had an early start to meet our friends. They were having breakfast when we arrived. Patty had insisted that they eat. Claudia told us that it was just what they were hoping would happen. They enjoyed Patty's meals. Dan and I were very happy to join them.

I phoned Eve before going to the Library. I told her we found our Hobby Horses and our racecars. She thought it would be nice sometime to bring the boys out to the Manor to see them. Max would like to see the old place again. He could watch the boys.

I knew I could not tell my lovely wife Eve what we uncovered. She was too close to Papa working with him every day. Each of us knew what the other was going to say before saying anything. I knew if she got upset, it would transfer over to him. So I just told her we may have found Charlie's where about. I told her to tell Papa that Dan and I would keep in touch.

Upon returning to the Library Kathy opened the Diary again and ignored the line about the pregnant girl. Kathy began to read the diary. "My mother's friend (Pauley) from up north ran a home for wayward girls. I had met him on many occasions with mother. Pauley was in love with her. Being related they could not marry. It was against the family rule. Whatever Veronica wanted he would see that she got it. They still managed to have a torrid love affair. Veronica used me to conceal their affair. Contacting him was the easy part. "

Margo asked if they could have a small break, she needed to use the powder room. They said they would continue when she returned.

After she left Kathy said, I think I prefer to translate what I read. Sometimes she refers to her mother, other times she calls her by name. I think she is nuts. She writes she told Pauley that the home in New York would be of interest to her. She knew of a girl that was pregnant. In New York, it would be easier to lose the girl than some place close to home. I did not want to read this in front of Margo after what she told us about losing her baby.

Margo returned and Kathy continued then she goes on about Emily's baby. She writes, "When Emily's baby is born it will still be too early for her own child to be born." She goes to New York on numerous occasions, telling the Staff she had information on Harry. This gives her an excuse to get her baby when it is born. Emily's baby was a few days old when she got word the other baby was due soon.

She had Pauley's driver go to New York with her to pick up that baby. He was a bit larger than Emily's fragile one but she would deal with that later. Pauley's driver got her home late at night. They gave the boy medication and he was fast asleep when they slipped him upstairs. When the nurse was not around, she switched them. She had to keep Emily sedated so she would not notice the change in her baby. It was a snap, putting Emily's baby in the freezer with his dear father.

Kathy said, "This is getting on my nerves, reading what this bitch has done." She writes that she received a call that a baby boy had arrived. She told the Staff that she was going to New York, saying there was more news about Harry. She had Pauley's driver pick her up. They headed for the airport but went up north instead. She returned with her son, Vinnie. Now I quote her. "Emily had died in her sleep (with my assistance. I really pulled that one off). I put on a good show of sorrow for 'Daddy'. Watching my 'Mother' do her stunts taught me how to adlib. Mother told me if you play it right, no one will trap you."

She writes that Charlie went on with his expeditions for the next ten years; leaving her in charge of raising the two boys. She pawned Daniel off on that stupid girl Molly. Vicky was furious when she discovered that Molly and Bert were married, right under her nose. She writes, I quote, "That bitch Annie had something to do with it. She never did like my son's name. Annie and that other bitch Louise wanted his name to be Victor. I told them Vinnie was my father's name. I never knew my father, but they did not know that" unquote.

Kathy put the diary down and said, "How about someone else reading this darn thing? I do not want to hog it myself." Claudia spoke up. "You are doing a good job, keep it up. If I take over I would spend too much time trying to decide what to leave out." Renee agreed, saying, she would only read the damn thing verbatim. They would be there all night. Therefore, Kathy picked up the diary and started again.

Vicky writes, everything worked out well until Charlie called one day and said he was going to have Daniel's name changed to Fargo. I guess I really flipped out on that news. As hard as I tried, I could not pretend I was happy. If Charlie guessed at my anger, well I would have to get rid of him too. I worked so hard for my inheritance and I did not want that brat to get any of it. I contacted Pauley and asked for his help. He taught me how to imitate Charlie's writing. I found out my mother was quite an expert at that feat. Charlie had written some letters on his last visit. I offered to mail them for him. (Yea in my own desk drawer.)

I was still practicing my skill when Charlie called to say he was coming home to see Edmond. I was still too shaky with the writing. I overheard Charlie ask Edmond if Annie made an arrangement with the Judge. When they came back home from the Court House, Charlie and Edmond went into the Library. I tried to follow but that bitch Annie wanted me to join her for coffee. After they left the house, I went into the Library. The papers were on Charlie's desk. I was furious when I saw it was a copy of his new will. He had left everything to 'Dan his ADOPTED SON'.

I knew I could prove that Emily and Daniel were not his blood heirs. I had no idea he was ADOPTING him. This left me no alternative. I had to get rid of dear "Charlie" before he died of natural causes, or had an accident.

Now was the time to show Charlie the bomb shelter He was late getting home from seeing Edmond. I waited up for him saying I discovered something unusual. I showed him the stairway. As he started down, I hit him hard on the back of his head. He fell down the stairs and I pushed him into the shelter. I gave a few more good whacks with the hammer to be certain he was really dead. His blood splattered just as Harry's did. Now I would have to paint again.

I called Pauley and again asked for his help in putting Charlie into the freezer. He was much bigger and heavier than Harry was. I also needed help in getting rid of Charlie's car. I wanted the Staff to see him leaving the house. Paul said he would arrange everything for me. (I had always thought he was under the impression that I was his and Veronica's child).

I called Edmond and told him Charlie received a call telling him that two of his men were working in a cave when it collapsed and received injuries. I also told him Charlie had to fly out immediately to help them. He had his plane ready and waiting for him to arrive at the Airport.

Pauley came with a man dressed to look like Charlie. I was surprised at the resemblance. I had to give him a second look. I called the Staff so they would see him leaving. Just as they were pulling away, Edmond and Annie drove up. The fellow in the back seat waved and Pauley drove on. I called to Edmond to stop and told him Charlie left him a note in the Library. Although the news shook Charlie badly he did manage to scribble a note for him. (That took care of my shaking hand). The note said he would call or write as soon as possible.

The actor practiced imitating Charlie's voice and actions from the movies Charlie made when Emily was born. I wrote what I wanted him to say when he phoned Edmond. The first call made a week later had Charlie sounding upset over what had happened on the site when the cave collapsed. This took care of any mistakes I made.

I used that actor to help me on many occasions. We went to various digs that Charlie worked on. Always making sure no one saw him up close, unless it was a new person. He signed in (I actually did the signing). I also used him to help me fill our bank accounts in Italy. He pretended to be Charlie but I signed the signature cards, out of the sight of bank employees.

I had him call Edmond on a regular basis, when I knew that both he and Annie would be out for lunch. He left messages. I had a girl working the office. I paid her to give me this information

Annie caught her one-day talking to me on the phone and transferred her to another office.

Eventually the actor became greedy and demanded money from me. Once more, I called Pauley. Not long after that, the guy had an accident, just like Charlie's personal driver.

I decided to meet my twin brother. He was not at all happy to hear from me. I needed him to make my bank deposits. I made him sign the cards in the bank. I forced him to do things for me saying I would tell mother that our father sold me to Veronica. This he said was not true and I could not prove it. He told me HIS mother had a bad heart and I would upset her needlessly. I told him if he did not want me to meet our family he had to do some small favors for me. The name Fargo seemed to have a special meaning to him.

Kathy stopped reading and began to turn pages. She said the rest seems to be about Vito and his dislike for her. It appears Vicky did not care what he thought as long as she got her way.

Kathy went to the end of the Diary and said this sounds interesting. Vicky wrote, quote. "This has been such a waste. I have spent the better part of my life draining Charlie's wallet and what did it get me? A family I do not want and a twin brother that wants nothing to do with me. I have a fortune I will not live to spend. I do not want that Monster Vinnie to have one more cent. Ever since he heard me talking to Pauley, he has hinted he knows more than I suspect. If Pauley were still alive, I would have him take care of that brat. The doctor said I have six months, more if I can take it easy. With that bloodsucker, wanting more money every month easy was impossible. He is too stupid to know about the secret room. I will write to my brother and tell him that Vinnie is not my real son. He is not a member of that family." Unquote.

Kathy said, "That is the end, she wrote no more." They just sat there digesting what they had just heard.

Claudia looked at Margo and shouted, "Margo, Margo you are white as a sheet. Quick somebody call a doctor."

148

Margo was sitting there crying. She gasped, "No I am not ill. I just realized Vicky switched my baby for Emily's baby. Dan is my son and I can not claim him or Papa Wilson will want to know how I found out."

Dan went to her side and said, "If you are my natural Mother, than Bert was my natural Father. Bert and Molly raised me. Now I can grow old with my Mother at my side."

Richard said, "we can fix it so you can call Margo, 'Mom'. We will all call her 'Mom', and then you will not need to worry about slipping in public and calling her Mom."

There was a knock at the door. It was Ida, the gardener's wife. She asked if we wanted coffee, or tea with sandwiches. Patty had sent her since it was past lunchtime. We thanked her for being so thoughtful. We would he better able to think of a solution after some refreshments.

***

All Matt could utter was, "Wow! That is something to discover. Did you and the others come up with a solution?"

"Patience young man, if there were no solution, we would not be sitting here. Enough for now, Jason was telling me about a movie and I want to see it. You and I will have some work to do at the office tomorrow. I am going to Chair a Board Meeting and I want you to sit in on it. Someday it will be your responsibility. We will resume our talk after that.

Matt and Alan returned home from the Board Meeting, but before they could enter, the den Emma had their dinner waiting.

"That was some dinner, do you feast like that every day or was that for my benefit?"

"Not to worry, Jason is a health nut. All our meals are for a healthy heart. He keeps Emma in line on that score."

"In that case I am glad of your offer for me to stay here, at least until you kick me out. I know you want to hear what we decided. So here goes."

"Before you start, I was wondering if you brought those horses home to your boys."

"No, they had their own, nicer ones I must confess. We did bring the racecars. Max set a track in our garden for them to have a good run.

To get back to the eight friends (we knew then we would be friends for life) deciding what had to be done about the bodies. First, we read Vicky's letter to her brother Vito. The one she did not get to finish. It was in the strong box. There were others, I guess she could not make up her mind and did not send them. As we went through the strong box, we found the baby's Birth Certificates. There was one for Vicky, one for Vinnie and one for Daniel Benson (Proof he was Margo's baby). There were pictures of people we did not know. One was a picture of a man with a young boy and Veronica. Written on the back was a notation stating Pauley's Godson.

After a long discussion, all eight of us agreed that Dan and I should go to Italy and talk to this Vito. Our discovery could destroy his family as well as ours. She was using him in her scheme to drain money from Charlie's accounts. The law would hold him accountable even if he did not know of the murders.

Dan and I planned to take a commercial flight. Eve talked to our Pilot and he had the company plane ready for us. We asked him if he had known Charlie's Pilot.

He replied, yes, but HANK was…suddenly…well Mr. Fargo stopped using that Jet. I do not know what happened to Hank. No word as to why, he just seemed to vanish from the face of the earth. Hank had flown for the Wilson family also. Max tried to find him but to no avail. Mr. Wilson provided his family with money to send the children to college. The housekeeper was puzzled. Hank had not come into the house for his usual coffee and pie.

I was without a job; I had been a commercial pilot. With my experience, and until Hank was found, I began to fly the company plane for the Wilsons. Now it is my pleasure to fly this wonderful plane.

Chapter 20
VITO

We arrived in Italy and rented a car to take us to the town where Vito lived with his family. (We did not tell the Pilot that we knew what happened to Hank).

Vito was not too friendly upon hearing we were from Vicky's hometown. He would not let us in to explain why we were there. We sat down on his porch to think.

His wife, ROSA, came out and ordered us to leave. We told her we were there to protect her family and ours from a crime that Evil Bitch Vicky committed.

Her son came out and sent her back into the house. He said he would hear us out. I gave him the letter Vicky had written to Vito before she died. We found it in her desk. FREDDO, the son, cursed the name and we nodded in agreement. That gesture seemed to please him. We explained what we found. She murdered three human beings. One was an infant. In all probability, she caused the death of her sister Emily. The infant was Emily's child. We found the body of Emily's husband

Harry and our Grandpa Charlie Fargo. His eyes lit up at the name Fargo.

We told him if that story ever got out; even though Vito did not know that he was helping Vicky mail letters from a dead man the law would still accuse him of the crime as an accomplice. It would not matter if we believed Vito did not know. The Law would not. The newspapers would have a field day. Freddo told us to stay on the porch while he explained things to his father and mother. The door opened and Rosa stepped out. We had not noticed the open window. Rosa and Vito were listening to us talk to Freddo. She opened her arms and said, "You boys look like you have had a rough time, come in and rest." She gave Dan a big hug. Vito extended his hand to me and then put it around my back giving me a warm welcome. Vito explained he did not know what was in the letters.

He asked what he could possible do to help. We said we needed a Death Certificate for Charlie Fargo dated two weeks before the bitch died. We would also like to find an unmarked grave and take a picture of it to show our Papa. If Papa knew what she had been doing it would kill him. We loved him too much to let that happen. There was nothing that could be done to Vicky or her son Vinnie as they were both dead.

Then we asked him why he denied being her twin. He said, "Because he was not. It is a sad story. My twin did not survive long after birth. Come, Mama fixed you two some dinner."

Freddo agreed, "You will eat for Mama even if you are not hungry! Mama makes everyone eat or she is not happy."

Eating in that house was a real feast. You did not need to be hungry to enjoy her cooking; it was delicious. We found them to be a loving family.

Vito told us he did as Vicky requested for years. She threatened to tell his mother that she was here. He said, "Mamma was ill with a heart condition, the doctors told us she was not to have any excitement. I could not take the chance of that woman getting Mamma excited. When I could not take it any longer, I told my oldest brother Dino. He said he knew about the baby switch. This was the first time I knew of it. He told me Mamma was so proud to be having twins. Mamma's health was frail at the time. The nurse at the hospital told Papa that she switched my sister for a baby born the same day. The baby's mother had left her in the hospital; she was not coming back. The nurse told Papa my twin would not survive the night. She said this poor little girl had no one to love her. Papa agreed to bury my sister in our family cemetery. He told my mother how bad he felt for the little abandoned baby. Her name was Victoria just like my twin. Mamma often wondered why Papa took flowers to that little grave so often. He said it was to remind him just how lucky they were.

When Veronica stole the baby, Papa thought the real mother came back to claim her child. He did not have the heart to tell Mamma the truth. The police tried to find her but that woman was too cleaver or wicked, no, she was just plain evil.

Vicky told me that Papa sold the baby to Veronica for money. I wanted to kill her. I knew my Papa would never do such a thing. We are not the riches family in Italy, but nor are we the poorest either. I was so afraid that if she carried out her threat to tell Mamma it would kill her.

My brother DINO told me that when Papa found the money, he gave it to the church; never telling Mamma where it came from. Papa lived with that knowledge for many years. The name Veronica was never allowed to be spoken in our home."

Vito's son Freddo came back into the room. He had been listening to us talk to his father. He agreed with us that we needed to do something and he wanted assurance that the bodies would never be found. We told him we had the means to do just that. He said he knew of a way to obtain a Death Certificate. We told him we had Vicky's Death Certificate" on us, along with her bankbooks, listing Vito as one of the owners. If he made a copy of Charlie's Certificate, his father could claim the money in the bank. It was several million dollars.

Vito said he would not take the money. We argued telling him he could use the money for something good. Perhaps the church or something else needed to help the people in their town. Freddo said his brother THEO would help his father to understand. He was the local doctor in town. Freddo was a lawyer and another was a priest. Vito was the Mayor.

Dan told Freddo that I was a lawyer. I told him I do not practice the Law. I barely got through Law School. It was by the skin of my teeth I finished. It was not my interest. I almost did not pass the Bar. I was more interest in Business Management. I went to school to get my degree in that field. It does help to understand the Law.

Vito's lovely wife Rosa called the family together for a feast. We were amazed at the size of the family. Each woman brought her favorite dish. There was so much food served, Mostaccioli, Meatballs, Litte Hats, tomato sauce, Baked Lasagna, and much more. Best of all was the Cannoli. They put the dinner together so fast we were in wonder. Not to mention how soon everyone appeared. We saw pictures of their Priest son ANGELO and his friend, DOMINICK.

Dominick was the godson of their cousin Pauley. She said Pauley had to move to America to get way from a cousin that was in love with him. There family did not allow this. They banished the woman from the family because she would not leave Pauley alone. We never mention her name because Mamma forbids it. I think she was a stage star. No one in our family ever saw her.

Vito and Rosas insisted we stay the night at their home. The next day we had a tour of the vineyard. THEO showed us his hospital. It could use an upgrade on equipment. Then we went to the church. The cemetery was behind the church. We noticed a small building at the rear. I asked what it was. Theo said it contained the remains of his long lost ancestors. An Archeologist found the remains up the hill and he brought them here to town. The man donated the building for them. His name is on the dedication plaque. He did not stay long enough to see the building finished.

We went to see it for our self. Sure enough, the name on the plaque read Charles Fargo in large letters. Theo called Vito over and told him this was the same man. Vito could not believe it.

Theo asked why we wanted a picture of a gravesite. We told him we did not want our Papa making plans to bring Charlie's body back. We were prepared to tell Papa that Charlie had a mistress that cared for him in his last years. One who loved him very much and brought flowers to his grave every day. We would convince him it would not be fair to her to disturb her grief.

Theo said his Aunt TESSA was about Charlie's age, he would tell her we were family of Charles Fargo and wanted a picture to show our family in America. Aunt Tessa was so obliging. She put on her Sunday best to pose with a large bouquet of fresh flowers. We took the picture, holding the flowers in such a way that only Charlie's name was shown on the building.

Theo supplied the Death Certificate. He said he would have it put in the records so it would be there if anyone were looking for it. That way there should be no question asked. We gave him Vicky's Certificate along with her Bank Books. We said we would destroy all of her mail from Vito and the letters she had written and did not mail.

The family wanted us to stay longer but we had important matters at home to take care of. Rosa and her daughter insisted we take some Cannoli home with us, we did not object. We were glad we had flown there in the company Jet.

I called Louise and told her we had proof to give Papa on what shocked him. I asked her not to say anything until we returned home. I then called Eve to let her know we found Charlie. Dan called Claudia and told her to let the others know that our mission was a complete success.

We drove the rented car to the airport where our pilot Bill and the plane awaited. We were in a much better mood then when we first arrived. We had a found new family, one we would treasure for the rest of our lives.

After we arrived at our airport, we got in our car and went straight to the Manor where Margo, Richard, Kathy, Michael and Claudia were waiting for us. We told them of the wonderful family we met in Italy. Claudia remarked at how much more relaxed we both looked. We both agreed that we felt fine; we had the answer to the main problem.

We showed them the pictures of Charlie's gravesite, a small building marked with his name. The woman in the picture was that of an aunt. We had the pictures Rosa gave to us of her sons and daughter. Last, but not least, were the Cannoli. Everyone sat and devoured those delicious treats. Margo said she had the recipe but no one could make them taste like those. She told us if we wanted more, we would have to go back to Italy and find Rosa.

Dan finished showing the pictures and then got back to business. Now we must convince Papa that the Death Certificate was in the papers he removed from Vicky's desk. That would account for the shock he received.

I called Louise and told her we were home. She whispered into the phone asking if Charlie was dead. I asked her if she was up to the truth.

She said yes but did not think Edmond was ready to hear it yet. She told me they were going out to the Ranch for a short vacation. After that trip, he may be able to adjust to

Charlie's death. Dan and I gathered the papers from Papa's Brief Case. We decided to use the letters he may have seen in there. We destroyed the forged writing of those evil witches, Veronica and Vicky. We inserted instead letters Charlie had supposedly written to her and Vinnie. We then inserted the Death Certificate and one of the envelopes with Vito's address. We destroyed all of letters from Vito and the letters she had written to him but never mailed.

We were prepared to show Papa the pictures of Charlie's grave and the woman that took such good care of him; knowing that Papa would be grateful that Charlie had someone in his life to care for him during his last days on earth. Then we would show him the pictures of Vito, Rosa and their lovely family. Dan said we could tell Papa of the vineyard, the church and the cemetery.

Now that the plan has been taken care of all eight of us felt a sigh of relief. There was nothing else to do but stop for the day and come back tomorrow. We all needed the time to think of what we had to do with the bodies in the shelter.

Chapter 21
HIDDING THE BODIES

Richard said, "We must find a way to hide the bodies in that room. What do you think of filling the damn thing up with cement?"

Michael volunteered an answer. "I know of a man that does that kind of work for a living. We can tell him we want to build on that spot but there was an empty room under the area. He can tell us how much cement we will need to fill it. I will have him over to see what he can do. We would not need to take him down to the shelter. We will just give him the size and show him the airshaft up top to see if it is large enough to pour in cement. Let us move the freezers to a position where they can not be seen through the shaft." We agreed to think on that and said our good night.

The next day we moved the freezers to the rear wall. Dan and I did it alone. Dan brought some flowers along for the baby. He said "Rest in peace little one in the arms of your father." I must admit tears began to flow from my eyes when I heard him.

We went upstairs and Dan was wiping the tears from his eyes. We cried for the needless death of that innocent child and his mother and father.

We still were not sure that filling the shelter up with cement would solve our problem. What if at some later date someone comes and digs up the ground? Kathy had an answer for that. Her idea was to build something that no one would desecrate. Margo suggested a Mausoleum with beautiful Marble for the floor and walls. Renee, Kathy and Claudia said they would start working on plans for a Mausoleum. They would start by going to various cemeteries to see what they have to offer. It will be helpful to take pictures of the different buildings.

While they were still deciding on plans, Dan and I took the papers from Papa's Brief Case to the office. Dan was trying to get into the file when good old Max showed up and wanted to know what he was doing. Dan told him he needed some letters in Papa's files that Charlie wrote. To change the subject he asked Max if he remembered the driver that always met Charlie at the airport when he was in the states.

Max said, "Of course I do. He disappeared right after dropping Charlie off at the airport. We finally found the car months later at the bottom of a ditch. It appeared that some truck ran him off the road. We investigated the accident for years. We never found Hank. The only concrete thing we came up with were some old truck parts that were disposed of in a salvage yard. The owner knew nothing of how they got there. The paint matched the car Hank was driving. We found witness that saw three cars on the day Hank was driving. After a long search, we discovered one of the cars belonged to a guy named Pauley. He had a bad reputation. We concluded that Hank's car was mistaken for one of the other cars. They killed him by mistake. This guy Pauley claimed to know nothing about the incident. Mr. Wilson wrote to Charlie and told him about Hank's death. Charlie wrote back telling him to take care of Hank's family. I read Charlie's letter, it sounded somewhat cold hearted to me. Mr. Wilson said that Charlie had to take care of some accidents at one of his digs.

Mr. Wilson saw to it that Hank's children went on to college and he took care of Hank's wife until she remarried. Not many knew about Hank's accident. Max asked Dan what brought that up. Dan said he saw a car that reminded him of the car he was in when Charlie adopted him. He just wondered what happened to the friendly driver. We thanked Max for the information and he said goodbye as he left the office. (So Pauley did have a hand in Hank's sudden disappearance).

My wife Eve came in and when she saw me she threw up her arms and nearly knocked me to the floor with her hug. She said, "I did not expect to see you until tonight." I told her I would be coming home alone tonight. Dan was staying at the Manor. Dan told her not to worry; Michael and Richard would be staying also.

She put her hands on her hips and said, "But I need Richard."

To that I replied, "You need Richard?"

She said "Not that way darling. I need all the expenditure records to pay the bills. Papa gave me permission years ago to handle the expenses of the Manor."

Max came back into the office to see what all the fuss was. We showed the Death Certificates to Max and Eve. Then she understood what caused Papa to have such a shock.

All agreed that we would wait for him to come home from the Ranch with Louise and Frank, before giving him the news. Eve said she talked to Louise before they left and Louise told her she had not seen Papa so happy and at ease since Grandma Annie's death. Louise said it may seem strange to tell but we all had the feeling that our Annie was right there with us, especially playing Bridge. Edmond said he felt her kick him under the table, then he would change his play.

When Dan and I returned to the Manor, they greeted us with a surprise.

Chapter 22
DOUBLE SECRET

The next day when Dan and I entered the Library, we saw Mike Mahoney at the large table, surrounded by Michael, Richard and the girls.

They were looking at the Blue Print Plans that lay before them.

Mike said, "Come on in, do not look so surprised. I have had a SECRET that will astound you. I have known about those bodies for a long time".

We would have collapsed at this revelation if we had not noticed the happy smiles on the faces of our friends.

He went on to say, "My great grandfather was the man that built this place for those shady people. He kept these plans and turned in a set to the building department without all the secret passages. He passed them down to my grandfather who in turn tried to give them to my father. My father put them into a pile for incineration. My father wanted nothing to do with them. I rescued the plans. I was sixteen years old at the time and inquisitive.

They discovered a tunnel when they started tearing down the farm at the far end of the property. I went into the tunnel to see where it led before they closed it off. It led to the Manor House. I guess you would call it an escape way for the gamblers. I reached the end; it was under the Grand Stairway. Not wanting some inquisitive boys, (he look at Dan and me) to come through and reach a dead end. I closed off the end in the Manor House. It was a tedious job. I could not use a hammer or electric drill. I predrilled the boards and brought them through the tunnel on a wagon. I had to screw the boards by hand, late at night."

Dan asked, "Just a minute, you said you saw the bodies. Why did you not call the police?"

My great grandfather turned in a false set of prints on the building. If I called, the Police there would have been an investigation into the secret passage. That would have implicated my family. They knew nothing about them. We are a peace, loving family; the press would have a field day dredging up the past. My great grandfather suffered for many years over this. He was in the grip of the mobsters that wanted the house built. In my family, I taught my children early on to only trust people that are honest and trust worthy. I could not bring this disgrace on my own children."

I asked him," When did you discover the bodies?"

"My Aunt Sara was the Head Housekeeper. I worked for Bert Benson as an apprentice in his carpentry shop. I helped him here at the Manor. Aunt Sara showed me the passage to the third floor. She said there had been a passage to the old wine cellar but someone closed it off by putting a door at the bottom of the stairs. She said it was there, not because someone was stealing. The stuff was not fit for human consumption. I was at that door one day in the wine cellar when I heard a man's voice on the other side. I could not hear what he was saying clearly.

When Vicky went on one of her trips, I managed to get the door ajar. That is when I found the Bomb Shelter, if that is what it is. I think it could have been a hideout for some of the mob.

I remembered working for Bert, when you (Dan an Alan) were young. I had many a meals in this house with the two of you"

Dan asked him, "Did Bert know about this?"

He replied no, no he and Molly were gone way before this.

When Michael ordered all those cinder blocks to bring to the basement, I figured you were going to cover up the evil deeds of that Witch. I offered my services to help Richard and Michael to bring the blocks in and mix the cement to cover the freezer chests. I understand that you are only protecting your families as I wish to protect mine.

Bert and I had uncovered the trap door with an elevator leading into the basement. We kept it in working order and secret from everyone. It is still in working condition. You just need muscles to pull on those chains. That is how we brought the blocks down to the basement. I told my men that you are building something in the old wine cellar.

I said, "I remember you now, it was so long ago. You helped build our Hobby Horses. You also played with us when we used our cars in the basement."

Richard had much office work to take care of. Eve had been on his back to get the paper work to her. The four of us worked to get those freezers covered in no time. Then Michael said he would have his friend over to see about filling in the whole room. I said I would like to see those Blue Prints. I wondered if they contained all the secret passages in the house.

Mike replied, "They are all here. We can close off the ones you do not want used."

I asked, "Where does this one lead to the one from the basement?"

Mike looked at it and said, "It leads to the old flower house, it no longer exist. We can do away with that one, for starters. First let's get that cement job finished; before someone comes snooping around."

I told Richard he had better stay at the desk and start working on those payroll sheets for Eve or we would both be in trouble. He agreed with me, saying, "She wants them yesterday!"

The rest of us went to the basement and Mike started to mix cement. Michael and I carried the cinder blocks into the shelter and placed them around the freezers. It took us no time at all to hide the freezers from sight.

***

"Well, Matt, I think I have revealed enough for today. We still have to keep up with training you to take over my assignments."

"Did that take care of your solving the problems?"

"No, young man, there is much more to tell you, just be patient. I will get to it in due time."

***

The next morning Matt asked Alan if he felt like getting with the rest of the story.

"Let's see, where was I? Oh yes!"

I asked Dan if Richard and Michael were staying with him tonight or did they change their minds."

He said." We will be here; the girls will be staying with Margo and Claudia in town. Mother Margo does not want anyone thinking we are having an Orgy with all of us staying in the Manor overnight."

Richard added, "I think she is already planning a triple wedding."

"A triple wedding?" Dan and I said.

Richard replied, "Yes I said a triple, Dan and Claudia, Michael and Renee and Kathy and I. The marriage Kathy and I had in Nevada was not a real marriage. I promised Kathy's mom that they would have a real wedding soon. We only married to protect her reputation while traveling across the country alone with a man. We do not consider ourselves married."

I nodded, since they were all going to be married as soon as this mess is over, why not all of us get married at the same time. I am sure Mother Margo will convince all six families to have the wedding reception here at the Manor House.

Soon it was time to clean up. Dan did not have a change of clothing. Michael offered him his, they were a little small. Richard's were slightly larger.

Mike said he would be back first thing in the morning to meet the cement contractor.

Going home that night without Dan seemed strange. We had been together nonstop for five or more days, I think, I lost all concept of time. It was wonderful to be with my boys and Eve again. Max tried to question me on what we were up to, he is relentless in his questions. I managed to dodge giving him any specifics answers. My boys helped me on that score. I slept well for the first time in days.

Before I left the house the next morning, I told Eve that Richard would have the paper work down by this morning. Upon arriving at the Manor, I saw a large cement truck pulling up. Michael and Mike Mahoney were directing the truck to the rear.

I entered the house and went straight to the Library. Richard was up to his ears in paper work. I asked where Dan was and he told me Dan was waiting for his pants to be dried. He could not wear Michaels or Richards. The girls were busy at the long table in the center of the room drawing up plans for the Mausoleum. I do not think they even noticed me coming in; they were engrossed in their work.

I had Dan's clothing and all the items he put on a list for me to bring back. I told Richard I would go and give them to Dan. We had breakfast in the kitchen. It was getting to be our daily routine.

Mike came in and asked if we wanted to see the work in progress. Out back, they had uncovered the air vent for the shelter. It was large enough to pour cement into the room. I wanted to know how we were going to pay for all of this work. Michael told me to go and see Richard. I did just that and found out that he had called Milo in California and told him. Kathy would accept the insurance money. She had a charity that was desperate for the cash.

There is half a million to spend from Vinnie's policy to cover up his mother's evil deeds. Margo said, "We discussed this last night. We will use it in ways we choose. I am going to give my Aunt and Uncle's farm. For a wedding present, Renee and Michael will get the land separating the Manor House and the farm. That property goes back quite a ways. We will have a very large place to build whatever we decide.

Dan suggested that perhaps the Johnsons would be interested in selling the Stables. Provided they would run it as usual, keeping it in their family. We could pay all of the expenses, that place meant so much to Charlie, Grandma Annie and the rest of the family. Maybe we can talk Papa into using Charlie's money to buy property. Dan said that was just a passing thought, perhaps we would come up with something better. Renee and Michael said they would like to build their Dance and Music Studio on the property or here in Midtown. Claudia said she, Kathy and Margo were discussing building a small Theater on the property, nothing big or elegant. We had many things to figure out, but first we need to contend with Papa. He was returning from the Ranch in a day or two.

Chapter 23
BREAKING THE NEWS TO PAPA

Dan and I prepared the papers to show Papa. The ones he was holding when he had his attack. It was not easy. We put the letters together with the papers that had no relevant issues to the matter at hand. We included the envelope from Vito's letter with the Death Certificate and a typed letter from Vito. The girls composed the letter using Vicky's old typewriter. Then Mike Mahoney signed the letter. It was difficult to crumble the corners of the pile the same way. Papa had clenched them with his fist. We did not think he would remember so we decided not to worry about that. The letter the girls composed went like this.

Dear Miss Fargo,

It is with deep regret that I must inform you of your father Charlie Fargo's death. As you know, he has been ill for quite some time. I wrote to you in an earlier letter explaining his health problems. You are aware that he has been living off and on in this town with the widow DeBartolo."

The past two years his health has been getting worse. It was his wishes not to let his friend Edmond Wilson know of his condition. He did not want him to worry.

Mr. Fargo has taken care of the widow DeBartolo's welfare. He promised her she could bring flowers to his grave because his entombment will be in this town. They were very devoted to one another. There is nothing more I can tell you. Please inform Charlie's family and friends of his passing and convey our deepest regrets. The widow does not want her address given out. She prefers to remain private. I have enclosed the Death Certificate. Sincerely, Vito

Mike Mahoney scribbled the signature of Vito. We were afraid Papa would recognize one of ours. Then we decided we should just type it.

When Papa finally came back from the Ranch, he went directly to Frank and Louise's house. We told him on the phone we had news of Charlie and wanted to come over to show him. He insisted we wait until the following morning and meet him at the office.

For the first time that I can remember, he did not say 'MY OFFICE'. This startled us both. When I told Eve, she was surprised.

We arrived at the office and found him sitting at his desk. We showed him the Death Certificate. He looked closely at the pile of papers and read the letter. Giving a sigh, he finally said, "So that Witch knew of this without telling us. I am not the least bit surprised."

To our amazement, it appeared as though he was taking Charlie's death in stride. He said he was glad that Charlie had found someone to look after him in his illness. He informed us he would leave Charlie in Italy to keep her company. He missed his Annie. He would not want anyone taking her far away from him. We were surprised even further with him saying he felt that he lost his Charlie long ago.

Even Annie had said Charlie did not seem to be the same man. Papa chalked it up to Charlie's reaction to Veronica's confession that night before she died.

Then Charlie's beloved Emily died. God only knows how he suffered. Even Annie thought Charlie's letters were cold. He said, "Every time Charlie called it was when Annie and I stepped out to lunch. The office girl took his calls."

Papa told Eve that he was going to stay with Frank and Louise for a little longer. He was relaxing for the first time since Annie left. Eve and I both knew he was at peace in the quite of their home. At our house, he would have to contend with our two little rascals. Not to mention, Max lived with us. Eve knew Papa tolerated Max and the boys because he loved them. Max talked non-stop. Eve and I learned to tune him out.

Papa called a meeting at the office for a reading of Charlie's Will. It was a long Will. He left the Three J Ranch in Matty's hands to take care of for Dan.

Dan wanted to tell Papa he did not want to accept the money. I knew he could not say so without Papa questioning why. I rushed Dan out before he became too emotional. We were working too hard preventing Papa discovering what Vicky had done.

'We had a Mausoleum to build.'

Chapter 24
PLANNING THE MAUSOLEUM

We returned to the Manor and had a meeting with all eight in attendance. Mike was still working the cement project. The cement had to dry before we could start the Mausoleum.

The girls were still busy planning the designs for the Mausoleum.

We told them of the reading of the Will. Dan insisted he could not accept the money. Margo reminded him that Charlie had adopted him as his son and heir.

Dan said," That was because Charlie thought I was his grandson, which I am not as you all know."

Michael told Dan. "We could use the money for a good cause, just as he Dan, had told Vito to do with Vicky's bank accounts.

Richard said, "Kathy will receive a quarter million or more from Vinnie's policy. They did not want that either. They are donating it to a good cause. Building this Mausoleum is indeed a good cause. It is a final resting place for innocent people.

Especially that little baby boy. He was not really Charlie's grandson either."

Margo said that at first she was going to sell her family's farm and donate that money. Now she wants to donate the farm itself. For the children to experience the animals in their natural surroundings what do you think about opening a small zoo or farm? Nothing too large; we could hire a retired farmer to give the children a hands-on experience. Maybe she could talk her aunt and uncle to help out. There would be no fields to plow, just the sheer enjoyment of showing the farm off to the children. Her aunt and uncle are not in need of anything. What they did need she would supply.

Renee offered the property that is between the farm and the Manor. It goes far back and ties up with the stables. The farm also ties up with the land next to the stable.

Michael added, "You mentioned that the stables are in bad need of repair. Do you know yet if the Johnsons will let us buy the stables? Providing of course they will continue to run the place for as long as they wish, including passing the option down to their children."

Dan said, "I remember mentioning that idea to someone. I go along with doing that. Now while the cement is drying, let us give it some more thought."

Richard said, "There is something else we should consider. What would you think about setting up a Foundation? I will look into the details. It would be for the benefit of the community."

We all agreed to meet the next day. It had been a draining several days for Dan and me. We were emotionally wasted. I went home to my family and collapsed. Eve put me to bed like a child. I slept for hours.

I learned from Eve that Papa was letting my dad Robert, handle the Estate of Charlie. While we are waiting for the settlement of the Estate, we had the insurance money from Richard and Kathy. With the cost of things, especially the marble the girls included in their plans, that money would be gone in no time.

Plans for a Foundation and the Mausoleum were well underway. The cement had dried and we were taking measurements for the foundation. Dan felt the urge to go inside and see what was keeping the girls. He later told me Margo was deep in thought. He offered her a penny for her thoughts. The answer she gave him he would not have been prepared to hear. She said, "I am having reservations on what we are doing. Can we live with ourselves when all this is over? Is this moral"

Kathy agreed, "We will be together for the rest of our lives knowing that we have concealed those bodies. How can we live with that knowledge?"

Dan told her he had an idea. When he was in Italy, Rosa told him something she learned from her son the priest. She said he told her, "Your thoughts are your own, and they belong to you and you alone. Your actions belong to God."

Dan told Margo, "I know it will be difficult for us, but remember what we are saving. The reputation of not one but three families that had no knowledge of what evil was going on. I do not think God would want punishment for innocent people. I will make you an offering. The last one of us will have the option of telling the world of the evil deeds of Vicky and Pauley, or that one will take the knowledge to their grave with them and explain it to God."

Margo said that she more than not would be the first to go, she would pray for the rest of us.

Dan returned to the outside where I was working with Mike. Not too long after that, a man dressed in religious clothing came into view, followed by the girls and Richard who had just returned from his meeting with my father Robert on setting up the Foundation. Claudia was pointing in my direction. Patty had the man by the arm and brought him over to us. Margo tried to introduce him but he was in such a hurry to get on with his business. We did not catch him name. He mumbled some thing that sounded like he had come to bless the place. He put on some garments and held a book in his hands. Then he began to walk around sprinkling water on the ground that we had measured for the foundation of the Mausoleum. Before we could utter a word, he began to speak in Latin. I did not understand him nor did the others with the exception of the gardener, Norman.

The man left as quickly as he appeared. We did not get a chance to question him. When I asked Norman what the man said, he told me the priest blessed the souls of the departed and prayed using the gravesite for the funeral of the departed prayer, "May they rest in peace."

I asked the woman where he came from. Claudia said he rang the bell and seemed to know why he was there. He looked familiar. They assumed we had requested his service.

Margo wanted to see the pictures in Vicky's strongbox. Sure enough there he was, standing with Pauley and Vicky. He is Pauley's Godson, a priest. Dan took a closer look at the picture and said he is one of the boys in the picture in Vito's house. Vito and his wife Rosa said it was a picture of their son and a fellow priest; the Godson of Rosa's cousin Pauley in America. Therefore, that was the connection with Veronica in Italy. She said she was on vacation but did not mention her relatives in Italy.

We wondered how that priest knew of the bodies, unless before Pauley died, he had given his confession to his Godson. On the other hand, maybe Vito's son contacted him and asked him to do the family a favor. That would explain his being here.

Renee asked, "You mean Pauley knew what she had done?"

Kathy said, "Of course, in Vicky's diary she wrote Pauley had helped her. He must have been in on it all along. If you recall, it was Pauley that supplied the actor to impersonate Charlie when they got rid of his car."

Margo wondered about that driver, the one that drove Charlie whenever he was in the States. He would have known that was not Charlie in the car.

Dan said, "Yes I remember him, he was a friendly person and so kind to me the day I was adopted by Charlie. I guess we forgot to fill you in on the driver's demise. It is all in the files in Papa's office. Hank supposedly had an accident. Papa took care of his family. That makes five people Vicky is responsible for killing."

Later I called Vito's son Theo in Italy to ask him about the visiting priest. He did not want to talk about it over the phone. He said he was coming to America to see his brother Angelo and would stop to see us before he left to go back home. He told me he would tell us what we wanted to know about them. He was anxious to see our plans for the Mausoleum. When at last he arrived, he solved the mystery for us. Theo said the priest was Dominick, his Brother Angelo's friend. Dominick told Angelo that Pauley had the gull to ask him for his last confession when he was dying. When Dominick graduated from High School, he came to live with us in Italy. His parents did not know of Pauley's mob connections when they asked him to be Godfather to their only son. Pauley started acting as if he wanted Dominick to go into business with him. This was out of the question for his parents. They did their best to keep him from Pauley's influence. He became a priest with my brother Angelo. Dominick told Angelo about Pauley's request. He said he could not bring himself to give that man absolution. Dominick prayed in Latin asking God to judge this man himself. Pauley did not understand Latin. He thought he was off the hook with God. (What a surprise he had in store for him on Judgment Day.) Dominick decided to bless the graves of the innocent victims of Pauley and Vicky.

We were relieved and grateful to hear this news. We had been worried about their internment in unmarked graves. In fact, Margo was so relieved she began to tell stories. She told of a bulletin article sent to her by a friend years ago. It concerned a priest in her friend's church.

This man gave the priest a case of fine wine, with the obligation to mention the gift from the pulpit on Sunday. He did this by saying thanks to the man for the grapes he gave and the spirit in which they came. Then she told of a saying her friend keeps posted in her kitchen. It goes something like. "To be cursed by the devil is to be truly blessed." She did not know the author. I am not sure I understand the meaning. She said it was a consolation for her friend. A jealous creature had maligned the woman's daughter. The daughter is doing well, not so for that evil creature with the Serpents Tongue.

***

Later that day Alan said to Matt "I have told you all you need to know. The future of the Park is now in your hands. What about your brother Pat?"

Matt answered," Pat really meant it when he said he did not give a Hoot about any secret. He is just thrilled to be a member of the Foundation. He loves his job."

"Well" then, there is no need for him to know the details. I did tell you about the pact the members made. Dan was sure he would out last me. When he became terminally ill, he asked me for my forgiveness. I told him I would pass this burden on to someone I could trust. That someone is you Matt. You decide what you do and not want to do, O.k. by me. Just telling you all the details have made me feel free.

Renee and Michael's three daughters are Members and they do not know of the secret. One is in charge of the Dance Studio, one the Music Department and the other the Theater."

Matt asked, "Who is in charge of the stables, wasn't that Dan's job?"

Alan said, "I know the perfect person for that position, if he will accept. Do you want to ask Jason or do you want me to?"

Matt answered, "I know Jason would like to hear it from you."

"Where has Jason been keeping himself these last few days? He has not been around here."

Matt said, I guess he is working on a Secret Project of his own, but it is getting late. We can call it a night. I will see you tomorrow."

Chapter 25
THE PERFECT SOLUTION

The next morning Matt turned to Alan and said, "What a beautiful day. Let us take a ride to the Mausoleum. Jason said he would be waiting for us. He has a surprise for you. He has been working very hard. I hope you will be pleased. Jason has taken care of our future.

As he drove, Matt asked, "How long did it take to build the Mausoleum? I would like to hear about that triple wedding. Did it take place? It has been such a pleasure listening to you these last few days in my den."

"The weddings took place within three months. The building took about five years before completion. It was not an ordinary building; the statues and the marble for the floor had to be special ordered.

Renee and Michael had three girls. First, they had twins, and the next year, they had the third. Dan and Claudia had no children, nor did Kathy and Richard.

By the time the Mausoleum was finished, Richard had the Foundation fully set up. Dan had turned the Ranch over to Matty's family. We owned the Stables and the buildings of the Theater, the Music Hall and the Dance Studio were completed.

Dan and Claudia redid the master bedroom suit, turning it into a small kitchen and sitting room. Margo went to live with her aunt and uncle for a year on the farm, which is now a petting zoo. Her aunt and uncle decided they liked their retirement home better. Dan and Claudia convinced Margo to move into the Manor House. Richard and Kathy had their own living quarters in the house. Renee and Michael built living quarters above the Dance Studio. That is when we decided we needed a full time maintenance man. This brought Jason into our lives. He has been another son to me all these years. He, Eddie and John got on as if they were truly brothers. They are the same, to this day.

At the entrance to the Manor, Matt turned toward the side with the Mausoleum. "Look, he said, do you notice a change? The first thing Jason did was to change that big door. He could not get the hang of that stupid lock. I did not get to tell him of the secret switch until after he had the door removed. I thought he would break my neck. He said he felt so foolish."

Before Matt could utter another word, Alan gasped. "What about the papers in the Pillar? Some vandals might break in and find them"

"Do not give it another thought. Jason took care of them. Just wait until he explains his handy work."

Alan gave a sigh and said, "It is a beautiful door, I must admit, but is it safe from pranksters?"

"Jason had an alarm system set up in the Manor. It will be monitored 24 hours a day."

Jason met them at the door, "Well it took you long enough, I have been wondering when you would get here, come see the changes I have made."

"Jason," Alan said, "If I have not made it clear before now, I want you to know you will become one of the Foundation Members."

Jason could hardly believe his ears. I have wanted to be a member for as long as I can remember. You hinted a few times that someday it would be my turn. I never know if I should take you seriously. You tease me so much."

"Then it is settled, attend the next meeting and familiarize yourself with your duties. You will be in complete charge of the Stables. I know you had been doing this with Dan for years. Since he passed on, you have done all the work. Now it is your official duty. When you, John and Ed were at the hospital, Dan asked me if I though you would accept the responsibility. I told him I would take care of everything. He was so upset that he was passing on before me. He had planned to be the last of the gang to go. I told him not to fret. I had made plans to pass our secrets on to someone trustworthy. It would be his choice to tell or not. I did not tell you sooner Jason because knowing how your mind works, I was afraid you would think you were pushing Dan out of the picture. I wanted to give you enough time to grieve his passing. You and Matt now have that decision to make I am free of the burden. O.K., show me the changes you have made!"

Jason told him he had removed the mechanism that operated the opening and closing of the lock on the door. Our Security system is in full operation. He then took his Uncle Alan by the arm and let him to the large Pillars at the far end of the room. He opened the secret latch hidden among the gold decorations and showed him his handy work. The door slid open revealing two beautiful Urns.

Alan Wilson stool with his mouth dropped and his eyes wide open. Turning to Jason he asked,"where are the Journals? The Diary of Vicky, that in it self would reveal all we tried to hid." "In the strong box is where they are along with Charlie's personal wallet and his identification cards," said Alan.

Jason replied, "I remembered Uncle Dan and you telling me when Papa passed away that he left instructions for you and Dan to have him cremated, just like Grandma Annie was. He wanted the two of you to ride the horses and sprinkle their ashes over the meadows that he and Grandma loved so much. The trophy room is where I found the empty Urns. I gathered all the Journals, folders, everything that was in that drawer and burned them. I filled the Urns with the ashes. I burned Charlie Fargo's personal items and Matt and I took two of the horses from the stables. We went to the meadow to spread the ashes as a token of good will. Look under this glass dome. I build it to protect the Urns. I engraved them. One Urn is for Charles Fargo and the other Edmond Wilson. The engravings read "May they rest in peace." We will now proudly put them on display.

He then led Alan to a large brass plate that hung on the wall. It was titled "Donors to the Park" The first name was Annie Wilson followed by Frank and Louise Ryan, next came John and Jake Fargo, Jody and a number of other names that were loved ones of the members of the Foundation.

Alan ran his fingers over the names as if looking for someone special. Jason turned him toward the pillar that will someday hold his plaque. On the very top was another plaque, it read, "In loving memory of Eve Wilson for her dedicated work and loyalty to the Park. A tear ran down Alan's cheek.

Jason put his arms around his Uncle Alan and took him to the Pillar of the Accountant. He said, "Try to move his fingers now." It did not work. Jason laughed and said, "I removed the mechanism for this one also. I sealed the opening to the Library. No one will ever find any secret passage again. I even closed up the one in the closet leading down to the kitchen. We do not want any of the children stumbling across them. We know from experience how inquisitive they can be.

We will have to enter the Mausoleum from the front entrance. Matt and I plan on having an open house once a year to honor the departed members of the Foundation."

Alan said, "I suppose you have my plaque all ready to put in place for me."

Matt and Jason yelled in unison 'NOT FOR MANY YEARS TO COME UNCLE ALAN.'

Alan tuned to them and said, "You have made the PERFECT SOLULTION." Why did not any of the eight members think of that? It is such a simple solution."

"Because all of you were too emotionally involved and witnessed the incidents first hand. We have no attachments to those memories, just our love for you.

We have taken down the old sign that read,' MAUSOLELUM' and are replacing it with one that reads, 'PARK MEMORIAL BUILDING'

Alan said, "Then I will take you up on your offer and move in with you both permanently. My sons let me know they do not want me to leave them my money. They have enough of their own. I will be able to get on with some projects that I have been meaning to set up.

First, there is the shelter in Midtown for abused mothers and children. Then, there will be a Day Care Center in the park for the employee's children. They can bring all of their children to work. After a nice healthy breakfast, a bus to take them to school and pick them up after school, and bring them back to the Manor. They can partake of the programs we have to offer. We will have trained caretakers to tend to the little ones. The parents then will not have to go hunting for them after work.

We could also offer a clinic in town for abused husbands. You know there are some of them too. There are so many things needed. I remember my Grandmother telling me of the time she had to let go of some of her Lawyers. She ran a very tight Firm. If one of the Lawyers were ever using dishonest methods to win their case, she did not want them working for her. She had learned that from Uncle Henry, the original owner of the Law Firm. He often said, "If one has to lie to win a case, the case is not won, it is stolen." I remember my Grandmother screaming at one lawyer because she was so angry. She asked him. "Why are you so sure of yourself to think that you can not be made a fool of? A man that lies and cheats on his wife during many years of marriage is an expert at fooling even you." Needless to say, she did not keep him in the Firm. They still have Lawyers dedicated to helping people taken advantage of by shady, shameless shysters.

Oh! Yes, we can do something about having a small Museum. In it, we will have Charlie's Uncle Jake and also Charlie's treasures from their Archaeological Expeditions. We can do something to upgrade His Grandpa John's Photo Gallery. The list seemed endless.

Matt and Jason looked at each other shaking their heads in disbelief. They wondered, would either of them have the strength or the energy to keep up with Old Man, ALAN WILSON.

GLOSSARY

NAME

ANGELO	Priest son of Vito and Rosa
ANNIE	Wife of Edmond (Papa)
AUNT DORIS	Margo's aunt
AUNT HELEN	Guardian of Edmond's (Papa) mother
BAILEY	Renee's parents
BANKS, RICHARD`	Retired finance officer of Park
BENSON MS.	Was secretary to retired Richard Banks, now Pat's Secretary
BENSON	Molly's future husband, not related to Ms. Benson Handyman for Park. Did many odd jobs.
BONATAELI	The family in Italy

BROOKS	Lawyer of Investment firm who left to become a teacher. He taught Edmond at the Boarding School and continued his interest in the investment Firm.
BURNS HARRY	Classmate of Emily/ she later married him.
COOK	Housekeeper for the Hastings.(loved both Matt and Pat but kept it a secret.)
CLAUDIA	Dan's wife
DALEY MARK	Employee of Park
DANA	Jason's cousin
DANIEL	Emily's baby
DINO	Son if Vito and Rosa
DOMINICK	Classmate of Angelo, Vita & Rosa's priest son
DYLAN , JACK	Fake named used by Vinee, Victoria's son
EVE	Alan Wilson's wife
EDNA	Renee's college classmate
EMMA	Cooks real name
FARGO DAN	Lifetime buddy of Alan Wilson
FARGO JAKE	Grand uncle of Charlie
FARGO JOHN	Charlie's grandfather
FARGO JASON	Charlie's father
FARGO JODY	Niece of John & Jake raised Charlie after Parents' death.
FREDDO	Another Son of Vito & Rosa
GRACIE RYAN	Grandchild of Frank & Louise

HANK	Loyal driver of Charlie, gone missing
HASTINGS	Surname of Pat & Matt
HASTING ARES	Wife of Greg, George's cousin
HASTINGS GEORGE	Husband of Avis
HASTINGS GREG	Cousin of George
JASON	Mentor of Pat & Matt
KAREN	Daughter of Frank & Louise deceased. Mother of their granddaughter Gracie
KATHY	Costume designer/ Richard's wife
LANGLEY MAREEN	Trouble maker
MAHONEY	Did carpentry work on manor and reorganized Cleaning, gardening etc.
MARTIN PETER	Loving grandfather of Pat & Matt
MATT	Forman of Dude Ranch
MAX	Private Investigator for Law and Finance firms.very dear to the whole family/
McDonald MR.	Loyal friend of Pat and Matt's grandfather
MICHAEL	Renee's husband
MILO	Former Insurance agent at local bank friend of Family
DR. & MRS. MILLER	Cared for Margo in New York after Vicky abandoned her in the home for unwed mothers.
MONIQUE	Aunt Helen's decorator
NORMAN	Gardner

NURSE TUDDLE	Friend of Sara (Friend also of Annie and Louise) kept them informed on what was going on at Manor house with Vicky
PAT	Matt's brother, in training as director of finance\ for the Park.
PAUL	Locksmith
PAULEY	Veronica's lover and crime member.
PHILIP	Sleezy Lawyer that Annie fired in her Law office
REGGIE	Innocent lawyer Philip blamed for his misdeeds
RENEE	Real estate agent and member of foundation
RILEY MOLLY	Helped Sara raise Daniel
ROBERT	Son of Papa and Annie
ROSA	Vito's wife
RYAN FRANK	Worked for Annie in Law firm
RYAN LOUISE	Papa's private secretary
SARA	Housekeeper for the Mansion Friend of Annie and Louise
SUSAN	Robert's wife
TESSA	Rosa's sister
THEO	Dr. son of Vito and Rosa
TIM	Tavern owner
UNCLE HENRY	Aunt Helen's husband
UNCLE HERMAN	Margo's uncle
VERONICA	Charlie's wife

VICTORIA	Veronica's daughter
VINNIE	Vicky's nasty son
VITO	Vicky's twin
WILSONS	EDMOND, ANNIE, ROBERT, SUSAN, ALAN, EVE, JOHN, RUTH & EDIE (Papa's family)